The Animals' Journey to the Moon

By Geeta Pati

Illustrated By G. L. Gustafson

ISBN: 1-886225-39-7

Library of Congress Cataloging-in-Publication Data

Pati, Geeta.
    The animals' journey to the moon / by Geeta Pati ; illustrated by G. L. Gustafson.
       p. cm.
    Summary: Happa the rabbit, Chalu the crow, Finny the fish, and Guru the owl journey to the moon, where they discover many scientific truths about the moon and space travel.
    ISBN 1-886225-39-7 (pbk.)
    [1. Space flight to the moon—Fiction.   2. Animals—Fiction.]
I. Gustafson, G. L., ill. II. Title.
PZ7.P27315An   1999
[Fic]—dc21

99-12683
CIP

DAGEFORDE
Publishing, inc.

Dageforde Publishing, Inc.
122 South 29th Street
Lincoln, Nebraska 68510
Phone: (402) 475-1123; FAX (402) 475-1176
email: info@dageforde.com
http://www.dageforde.com

Printed in the United States of America

10 9 8 7 6 5 4 3 2 1

Dedicated to my mother from whom I learned many invaluable lessons of life. I will always treasure them in my heart.

CONTENTS

Acknowledgements

I am very thankful and grateful to Dr. Donald Wentzel, an astronomy professor at the University of Maryland, for science-editing my book. I thank NASA for their generosity in providing most of the photographs and Palomar Observatory, especially Ms. Patricia Orr, for providing me with a number of beautiful photographs of the sun.

I would also like to convey my thanks to my husband— Jogesh— and my children— Sangeeta, Buno, Sushma (daughter-in-law), Shibani, Aarif (son-in-law) and Devesh— who have supported me wholeheartedly towards writing and publishing this book.

Geeta Pati

Author's Note

The Animals' Journey to the Moon is a story that teaches space science to children in an interesting way. This book is written to popularize space science among children ages 10 and above, and for the general public. In this space age, it is very important for children to be exposed to the achievements in space science and technology. Teaching science to children is not an easy task. Even though there are a number of pure science books on the market and in the libraries, most children avoid reading these books because they appear boring and monotonous to them.

All children love to read story books. From my experiences teaching my own children as well as working as a volunteer teacher in area schools, I found that children are much more receptive to science when science is presented to them in story form. Considering this, I have combined science with story in this book. I hope this will encourage children and young adults to read it as a story book and learn science.

In The Animals' Journey to the Moon, three animals— a rabbit named Happa, a crow named Chalu and a fish named Finny, along with their advisor, an owl named Guru— journey to the moon during the Apollo 11 moon mission. The three animal astronauts had no knowledge of the moon or space and they were not properly trained for the moon mission. During the space travel and while on the moon, these three animals learn scientific truths about space travel and the moon through their adventures and the explanations of the wise owl. These three animals are like children who are curious to learn, and the wise owl is like a teacher who is trying his best to teach them. The story is fictional but the science explained by the wise owl is true. I hope this book will prove to be enriching as well as entertaining for children.

In a sequel to this book titled Finny's Voyage through the Universe, Finny the fish travels through the universe and learns about wonders and mysteries such as: the Big Bang explosion, black hole, neutron star, nebula, nova, supernova and many more.

Chapter 1

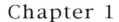The Conference

Deep in the rain forest of the Amazon, the animals of the world held a conference. It was a clear night early in July of 1969, and a full moon was hanging in the night sky. The president of the conference, a lion named Raja, stood proudly in the middle of an open glade, ready to address the wild audience. The place was packed with animals from land, water, and air. The chitter-chatter of the animals filled the night's sky. The animal representatives from each continent sat in the front rows: the giraffe from Africa, the kangaroo from Australia, the bison from North America, the panda bear and the Royal Bengal tiger from Asia and also the Polar bear from the Arctic region were among those present. It was a very important event for the animal kingdom.

Raja glanced around, ran his paws through his bushy beard, cleared his throat and started with a loud roar, "Silence, Please!"

Everyone stopped talking and turned their heads towards Raja.

"At present," Raja began, "the animals of the world are threatened with a serious problem. You should know that in 1958, a group of men in America founded an organization called the **National Aeronautics And Space Administration— NASA** for short. NASA studies and explores space, including all the stars and planets. NASA has many branches around the United States. One of its branches is in Florida. According to our number-one spy, Mr. Samu the eagle, NASA has made all necessary arrangements for humans to set foot on the moon. They're traveling to the moon in a rocket that will take off from **Cape Canaveral (Cape Kennedy)** near Cocoa Beach in Florida.

"As you probably know, humans needed our help to succeed in their early attempts at space exploration. A few years ago, men in Russia chose our sister, a dog named **Laika**, as the first astronaut and sent her up on their space mission. Similarly, men in America chose our sister **Ham**, a chimpanzee, to be a space explorer. We, the animals, shared the human success and victories in outer space. We were like their partners in space exploration. But now, the story is different. Men have decided to brush us aside so that they can be the first living beings to set foot on the moon. It's so unfair— they haven't even *considered* us animals. What an outrage! To me, this sounds like a conspiracy of men against animals." Raja was furious, and his mane waved wildly in the night air.

"Look at the moon," he continued, pointing overhead. "This bright and lovely moon shines on us too. We have as much right to pay a visit to the moon as men do. While men sleep, the silvery moon shines on our animal kingdom, lighting our paths and making our lives easier. Can you think of anything more humiliating to us than having men get to *our* moon before we do? Those humans think they can be the first to succeed at everything! Well, what do you think, my friends? Who should be the first to set foot on the moon? Them, the men? Or us, the animals?" the lion paused.

A loud uproar rose from the animals. "We should be! We want to be the first to set foot on the moon! Not men! Not men!"

"Good thinking! Let's all join paws and work together. We must win this race to the moon."

The lion finished his speech to a thunderous rustling of wings and clapping of paws. Soon the jungle was filled with the whistles, barks, and howls of the jubilant animals. Without further delay, the clever fox, Mr. Vim, was assigned to choose the astronauts. Hundreds of animals came forward for the astronaut post, and each one recited the same sentence with great enthusiasm,

"I want to go the moon...I want to go to the moon!"

Mr. Vim designed a screening process to select the astronauts. First, he asked the candidates many questions about their early adventures and heroic activities. In the presence of the other animals, Mr. Vim tested each candidate on their strength, courage, physical fitness and other special talents which he considered important for an astronaut post. In the end, he chose three astronauts for the moon mission from land, water and air: Happa Hooper the rabbit, Finny Flapper the fish and Chalu Chacha the crow.

"Friends, I've chosen the astronauts," Mr. Vim announced. "I would like to present them to you right now. Meet Ms. Happa Hooper, a rabbit. She has been chosen as one of the astronauts to go to the moon. Ms. Happa Hooper is a highly qualified young female. She is physically fit, very intelligent, and a champion high jumper! Most of all, she is extremely daring! She will explore the land areas on the moon.

"Now, our second astronaut is Mr. Chalu Chacha, a crow. Chalu means "clever" in India. He is healthy, strong, a super flyer and a daredevil. In a daring attempt to save the lives of some baby birds, Chalu was crippled in one leg. But that didn't disqualify him from becoming our astronaut! Mr. Chalu is going to explore the moon's atmosphere.

"The third astronaut chosen for the trip is Mr. Finny Flapper, a fish. He is a very special fish! He can live inside salty ocean waters, the sweet waters of the rivers, and also the muddy waters of the swamps. The most amazing thing about him is he can also live on dry land or underground for years without any difficulties! He has all the qualifications I was looking for to be an astronaut. He is going to check out the water regions on the moon. Let's give all our astronauts a big hand!"

Thunderous clapping of wings and paws flooded the jungle.

"Now listen carefully, my friends," Mr. Vim said to the animals. "The easy part is over. Now comes the hard part: figuring out how to get to the moon. We need transportation and many other necessary pieces of equipment to travel in space. In my opinion, we don't know anything whatsoever about the moon or space. What we need is some expert advice and the help of a counselor whom we can trust. To my knowledge, there's one such being who can help us. He is wise, knowledgeable and he's also my good friend, an owl named Guru Maharaj— Guru for short. He lives in the backyard of the director of NASA's Spaceflight Center in Florida. Mr. Guru is famous for his superior intelligence. He's also overheard quite a few important discussions among NASA scientists who visit the director. Yes indeed, he is one-of-a-kind, second-to-none in the animal kingdom! I'm absolutely sure he wouldn't hesitate even for a moment to lend a helping hand in our space mission. I think we should extend an invitation to Mr. Guru from all of us, requesting him to join us here," Mr. Vim concluded.

President Lion immediately ordered Mr. Samu the eagle to fly as fast as he could to Florida with an invitation to the wise owl. Mr. Samu, being a competent spy for years, knew exactly where to find Mr. Guru. He said good-bye to the rest of the animals and flew off at once.

Chapter 2

Wise Owl, the Counselor

In a few days, the eagle returned to the woods with the wise owl, Mr. Guru. The animals were excited and overjoyed by his arrival. To welcome him, the animals built an entrance gate with multi-colored leaves and flowers. They showered orchid petals on his path and greeted him with bouquets of fragrant flowers and bunches of exotic fruits from the rain forest. Groups of animals and birds danced and sang sweet melodies to entertain the wise owl.

The wise owl was quite pleased with the overwhelming reception. He smiled a bit, pulled his glasses closer to his eyes and spoke,

"I am truly touched by your hospitality. It is an honor to be invited here as your counselor. I admire your great effort to journey into space! First, I must congratulate you on your astronaut selection. You have done a great job by choosing a female astronaut to go to the moon. She will be the first female to set foot on the moon in the history of animals as well as humans. Also I admire you for selecting a handicapped crow as an astronaut for your space mission. The handicapped shouldn't be disqualified for any kind of job if they are capable of doing it! So friends, for the first time in the history of space exploration, you will be sending a handicapped astronaut to the moon. I am really proud of you all and I will certainly be more than happy to assist in every possible way towards the success of this mission."

The animals applauded.

"But," continued the wise owl, "we must realize one crucial fact. We have a serious time constraint and this will be the biggest obstacle to our success. To get to the moon, we need to build a spaceship, train our astronauts and make numerous preparations crucial to a successful space mission. The humans have a big head start. They've spent years conducting space research, building their spaceship, training their astronauts, and making all other preparations for their space mission. In my opinion, our ambition to venture to the moon is a dream— one that will not come true unless we seek the help of humans." Before the wise owl could proceed any further, a tremendous uproar arose among the animals.

"Boo...No way...Never! Absolutely not!"

"Trust me, my friends! I do sympathize with your feelings," continued the wise owl, "but in my judgment, this is the only way we're ever going to get to the moon. Think in these terms: men in their early attempts at space exploration needed our help and cooperation and we generously offered it. Our sisters, the dog and the chimpanzee, helped them out. Now it is our turn to ask for their help and cooperation. Even if we aren't the first to set foot on the moon, we'll still be contemporary pioneers with humans. Think it over, but be practical and decide quickly, before it is too late to do anything!"

As Mr. Guru ended his speech, a big commotion arose. Heated arguments and discussions rumbled through the audience for several minutes. Finally being unable to arrive at any other feasible solution, they all agreed to Mr. Guru's proposal. The decision had been made and the session ended.

Mr. Guru encouraged the animals by assuring them that the director of NASA loved animals and he was a close friend of Mr. Guru. So the director would be more than willing to help them achieve their goal. Mr. Guru was sure that he'd have no difficulty in getting his human friends to help him and the animals build their own spaceship and prepare for their space journey. He also agreed to accompany the three animal astronauts on the journey as their counselor.

"What about the astronaut training?" asked Mr. Guru. "It's a very important part of this space mission."

"Don't you worry, Mr. Guru," said Mr. Vim. "You have your hands full with the arrangements for the space mission. We will look after the training of our astronauts and inform you of their progress from time to time."

"Do you know what kind of training the astronauts need for their moon mission?" asked the wise owl.

"Of course we do!" said Mr. Vim with confidence. "They need to be trained in water, in air, and on land. There is no other place but land, water and air!"

"That will be a great help and I believe that the natural environment is the best place for training astronauts," said the wise owl. "But there is some special training which can't be given to the astronauts in the woods. So you go ahead and train the astronauts the best possible way you can but keep me informed about their progress. On that basis, I will decide their future training." The wise owl bade farewell, promising to send Raja the lion a letter with all the final details on the mission. Then Mr. Guru flew off for Florida with Mr. Samu, the eagle.

In Florida, Mr. Guru met with the director of NASA and they discussed the animals' moon mission. The director was delighted to hear about the animals' space mission and showed his full support. But he couldn't make the final decision all by himself because it was an important decision. He had to consult with the other high ranking officials of NASA to grant permission for the animals' trip to the moon. So he made a plan with Mr. Guru about how to convince these officials to agree to this project. He decided to have a meeting of the high ranking NASA personnel. He helped the wise owl to invite the members of animal-lover societies, equal rights leaders, women's organizations, senior citizens' associations, and the handicapped and disabled organizations to the meeting. He told the wise owl that the support of the members of all these organizations would definitely help NASA officials to make up their minds in favor of the animals' space mission.

The meeting was arranged and the session started. The wise owl put forward the proposal of the animals' space mission at that meeting.

"The animals walked the Earth much before men!" said one member of an animal-lover society. "So they have the right to go to the moon! All these years, the animals have helped us in many different ways like true friends! It's about time we help the animals in achieving their goal because we owe it to them!"

"Yes! Yes! We support it fully!" an uproar arose from the animal-lover groups.

"Yes! This world is shared equally by all; men, women and animals!" said one equal rights leader. "All have an equal right to live their lives to the fullest and to realize their potential to the fullest! Who are we to deny that right to others? So let's help the animals in their space mission."

"The animals have shown us a great example of equality by hiring a female astronaut to set foot on the moon!" said one member of a women's organization.

A zero-gravity environment frightened the moon-bound animals. (see page 14)

The animals' space walk. (see page 30)

"The disabled should be hired as our animal friends have done for their space mission," a loud voice came rolling out of the handicapped organization. "We should and we must extend our helping hands towards the animals in their great attempt to support the disabled."

"Most of all, Mr. Guru, a senior citizen, is heading the mission!" said the director of NASA. "Mr. Guru is highly respected for his wisdom and knowledge. Moreover, he is mentally and physically fit to do anything! He is a great example of courage and daringness for all the seniors and for us as well, because sooner or later we will all reach that stage. So, let's help the animals in their space mission."

"Seniors should be supported fully if they are fit and willing to do the job. Anyone can make a difference at any age!" said one member of the senior citizens' associations. "

"We fully support it! The animals have done the right thing by choosing a senior for their mission! NASA must help the animals!" an uproar arose among the senior citizens.

The NASA officials couldn't oppose or reject the project because of strong support from all these important groups. After lengthy discussions and consultations, all the members supported the animals' space mission and they voted unanimously to go ahead with the project.

Mr. Guru, the wise owl, worked hard with NASA's engineers and technicians to construct a small version of **Apollo** 11, the human astronauts' spaceship. He named this spaceship, *'Puspaka,'* after a flying chariot in the mythology of India. He also had NASA make small **space suits** and **life-support systems**— just the right size for the animal astronauts— and he chose special space meals for himself and the three animal astronauts. Finally, NASA granted the animals permission to launch their spaceship on July 16, along with Apollo 11, the spaceship of the human astronauts.

When all the preparations were made, Mr. Guru asked Mr. Samu the eagle to deliver a letter to Raja. In the letter, he wrote all the details of the space mission including the departure date, time, and place. He asked the animals and their three astronauts to come to Florida as soon as they possibly could. Mr. Samu flew back quickly to the animals and handed the letter to Raja, who read the good news aloud to the gleeful animals.

The three animal astronauts, Happa Hooper the rabbit, Finny Flapper the fish, and Chalu Chacha the crow, set out for Florida along with their friends and relatives. Not realizing the urgency of their early presence in Florida, they traveled leisurely, taking time to visit new places and have fun. They stopped in Mexico and Chalu the crow bought some shiny silver cufflinks and a sombrero (Mexican hat). Then, Happa the rabbit hopped over to the desert to visit her cousin Jackie the jackrabbit. Next, Finny the fish stopped for a swim in the Gulf of Florida. Then, all three decided they had to take a detour and stop at Disney World. Before they knew it, it was the day before they were supposed to take off for the moon! They had to hurry as fast as their legs, wings, and flippers could carry them, and they didn't get to NASA until later that night.

All this time, Mr. Guru never heard from the animals about the progress in their astronauts' training or their time of arrival. He was very worried and anxious. When he heard the animals had arrived, he flew to their hotel to meet them. He opened the door to their room and couldn't believe his eyes. He found the animals dressed up in strange costumes. They were having a wild celebration. It was a crazy scene! The funniest looking band he had ever seen played in the corner. Two lizards wearing sunglasses banged on a big Congo drum with their tails while an octopus played the piano with all eight of his arms. A fat raccoon in a black beret made deep, soulful sounds on the saxophone, while a bear dressed in a suit covered with shiny old coins played the guitar. The animals in the audience made almost as much noise as the band. They were whistling, singing, and snapping their fingers, dancing and twirling around the hotel room. Two monkeys swung from the chandelier and one of them almost knocked Mr. Guru over as he stood gaping at the crazy scene from the doorway.

"What's going on here?" Mr. Guru shouted, "Is the circus in town? Because you certainly look like a bunch of clowns! I can't believe this, really! I can understand a bit of excitement, a little celebration over the upcoming moon trip, but this is absurd! You are making our moon mission look like a joke!" Mr. Guru turned towards the three animal astronauts and said, "You all have no sense of time! You have arrived here days later than I requested in my letter. On top of that, you had to throw this crazy party! Do you realize the consequences of your late arrival? I guess not! Let me fill you in," Mr. Guru smoothed his feathers a bit and continued. "By your late arrival, we have missed many important meetings and astronaut training sessions. What's going to happen if we have any serious problem in outer space? What will you do then, play your drums? Space travel isn't a game, you know! It's serious business, and don't you forget it. Now, you three astronauts come with me! I will take you to your assigned quarters where you can get some sleep." Mr. Guru turned towards the wild crowd and said, "The rest of you break it up and go home!"

He led the three animal astronauts to their quarters and said, "Tomorrow will be a very important and memorable day for all of us. You need to get ready early and be at the launch site on time!" The animal astronauts promised that they wouldn't be late and bade Mr. Guru good night.

Chapter 3

Takeoff

Under the clear blue sky of **July 16, 1969**, a historic event was in progress at Cape Canaveral (Kennedy), Florida. Apollo 11, a huge rocketship that stood 32 stories high, rested on its launchpad next to the tall red **gantry** (a steel-frame structure). Clouds of white smoke billowed into the air around the base of the rocket. A few hundred feet away, the animals' little spaceship, *'Puspaka,'* stood on its launchpad ready to take off for the moon.

That day, the fields and the beaches surrounding the launch site were crowded with spectators. In the crowd, there were: television reporters, cameramen, radio broadcasters, photographers, journalists, and important people from all walks of life. All of them competed for the best view of the Apollo 11. Everybody was busy scribbling notes and taking pictures of the historic event.

The nearby bushes and trees were packed with animals and birds from far and near. They all were curious and excited to see what would happen. Their eyes were anxiously fixed on the two spaceships.

In the meantime, the three human astronauts, **Edwin Aldrin, Michael Collins**, and **Neil Armstrong**, were getting ready for the trip in a dressing room called the *'Ready room.'* They were busy putting on their **space suits**, **helmets** and **boots** and were undergoing last-minute doctor's checkup before taking off.

Mr. Guru, the wise owl, was anxiously awaiting the arrival of the animal astronauts. He couldn't stop watching the clock on the wall. It was almost time for take off and still there was no sign of Happa Hooper, Finny Flapper or Chalu Chacha. Mr. Guru was getting very nervous.

"Where on Earth are they?" Mr. Guru muttered.

He couldn't wait any longer. Just as he picked up the phone to call their quarters, the three animal astronauts came rushing in, sweaty and breathless. They were buried with bags and suitcases from their heads to their toes. They

A view of the moon's crater from the animals' spaceship. (see page 36)

The crow attempted to fly on the moon, but he fell to the ground. (see page 41)

could barely walk. What a scene! Before Mr. Guru could utter a word, Finny the fish started speaking.

The animal astronauts with their luggages

"Sorry for the delay, Mr. Guru, but it couldn't be helped. You see, it took us a while to pack all of our stuff and carry it over here. It wasn't easy, not even for an agile guy like myself!"

"What kind of stuff did you bring?" Mr. Guru asked with surprise.

Finny replied promptly, "We brought our favorite snacks to eat on the way. I brought a big can of dry, crunchy bugs. Mmm, mmm, good! Happa has a bag full of garden fresh carrots, picked by herself. Chalu here has a sack full of fruits, corn and barley. Dee-li-cious! Besides—" before Finny could continue, Chalu the crow took over the sentence.

"Besides all that, we also brought our sleeping bags, tents, drinking water, a Monopoly set, a ball, and a guitar. Boy, oh boy! We're going to have so much fun!" Chalu continued babbling. "Better to be safe than sorry, I always say. It's very difficult to pack when you're going to the moon. Who knows what we may or may not get at the other end. Don't you agree, Mr. Guru?"

Even though Mr. Guru was upset, he couldn't help bursting out into laughter. "You three are real clowns! I can't believe it!" Mr. Guru said while laughing. "Where exactly do you think we're headed? Eh? A summer camp? An amusement park? An outdoor expedition, perhaps? Then after reaching there, are you going to pitch a tent, spread your sleeping bags under the sun, munch on your favorite snacks, play rock-n-roll on your guitar, or bounce your ball? Besides, how do you think you are getting there? In a jumbo jet perhaps, with enough room to dump all your stuff and stretch out your paws and wings? Am I right?" Mr. Guru said. "Come off it fellows! Let's be serious and get down to the facts. The truth is, you are going on a mission to the moon, a distant and unknown world never before visited by any living thing. Our carrier is a small spacecraft, barely big enough to carry the four of us in sitting positions most of the time. So, there is no room for all this stuff."

"But Mr. Guru, we saw the spaceship outside. It's huge; taller than a 32-story building. Why, there should be enough room in there for thousands of animals like us and tons of stuff like ours!" Chalu replied.

"Oh, no!" Mr. Guru laughed. "You saw Apollo 11, the spaceship of the human astronauts. I wish you astronauts had got here sooner so I could have shown you around and explained everything. Then we wouldn't be having all these problems. Anyway, I'll fill you in quickly. Apollo 11 is 360 feet tall, taller than the Statue of Liberty in New York City! However the astronauts' living space is only 10 feet 7 inches tall— the same size as the inside of a station wagon. The capsule consists of a small kitchen, two bedrooms behind the couches and a toilet. The cupboards are stuffed with packages of food, drinking water, fire-resistant clothing, personal-hygiene kits that include toothbrushes, combs, soaps and other necessities for the journey. Moreover, most of the walls are lined with instrument panels. As you can imagine, the astronauts' living space is pretty cramped.

"Our spaceship is an exact replica of Apollo 11, with a few minor variations. It's built to accommodate four animals of our sizes. We have exactly the same facilities as the humans, but they're scaled down to our size. So, even though we're much smaller than humans, we have just as little room in our spaceship as the humans do in theirs. Unfortunately, this means we won't be able to fit any of this stuff you've brought. So, throw away your stuff and follow me!"

Mr. Guru glanced quickly at the wall clock and exclaimed. "Good grief! It's almost time for take off! Let's go!" Mr. Guru flew off in a hurry. The three other animals put their bags down reluctantly and followed him.

It was already time for the countdown to begin. The animal astronauts didn't have time to put on their space suits, so Mr. Guru decided they would carry their space suits and life-support boxes along with them. The animals rushed into a van that drove them to the launchpad. As soon as the van stopped, they rushed out and ran into an elevator. The elevator took them up to the top of the launch tower to their spaceship. The animal astronauts got into their rocketship as fast as they could.

Meanwhile, the three human astronauts were waiting inside Apollo 11, dressed in their space suits. They were busily checking out the instruments and switches on the control panel, as mission control instructed. The animal astronauts were also sitting in their spaceship, 'Puspaka,' ready to take off, though they still hadn't had time to put on their space suits.

Then, before they knew it, the countdown began. An ominous silence spread through the crowd. A deep voice from mission control came booming out over the loudspeaker, "T minus,

"Ten...Nine...Eight...Seven...Six...Five...Four...Three...Two...One...Zero ...LIFTOFF!"

At that, the rocket engine of Apollo 11 was ignited and it blasted off from the launchpad. The rocket made a deafening roar as it rose from the launchpad and the Earth shook with the force. Enormous clouds of white smoke and orange and red flames shot from around the base. The spectators in the crowd held their hands over their ears and their eyes got bigger and bigger as they watched the rocket launch gracefully into the sky. The animals' spaceship, 'Puspaka,' also took off the same way. They climbed upward into space, with streaks of flame and wispy white smoke trailing behind them. As they soared higher, only the red and orange fiery end of Apollo 11 was visible from the ground. A few minutes later, the exhausted fuel tank, which looked like a flaming end of the rocket, was separated and fell into the ocean as the spacecraft kept on climbing and slowly disappeared from the audience's view. The little spaceship of the animals raced up into the sky beside Apollo 11.

In the tiny spaceship, the animals were trembling with fear and excitement. The acceleration of the spacecraft was creating a tremendous pressure inside the cabin. The four moon-bound animals were flattened like pancakes against their seats. The pressure inside the cabin increased even more until it was four times stronger than the gravitational pressure on Earth. They felt heavier and heavier every minute and they couldn't move a muscle no matter how hard they tried. Happa couldn't twitch her whiskers, Finny couldn't move his fins, and Chalu couldn't rustle a single feather. Their paws and wings felt like they were made of lead. It was especially confusing and unbearable for the fish, the rabbit, and the crow, who hadn't anticipated anything like this. It was a noisy, shaky and jerky ride. They imagined a trip in a rocketship would be like a ride on a roller coaster, but they couldn't have been more wrong. This wasn't fun at all! Just as they thought they couldn't take it any more, the spaceship reached **Earth orbit** and began traveling around the Earth at a steady speed. Within moments, the cabin pressure had returned to normal and the animals felt relieved.

"Mr. Guru!" Chalu gasped. "Taking off in a spaceship is not fun at all! It felt like someone put a piece of heavy rock on my chest and I was being crushed! I couldn't breathe! I was gasping for air! On top of that, the deafening sound of the rocket engine and the buzzing, clattering noises of the spacecraft made things even worse! The continuous rattling noise of the spacecraft felt like someone had put a steel pot over my head and was banging on it with a spoon! I've never heard such a racket! My ears are still ringing!"

"It's true that the pressure in an upward bound spacecraft is tremendous! Its intensity can vary from 2 to 8 times more than Earth's gravity, depending on the speed of the spacecraft. It takes your breath away and it feels terrible, but unfortunately, it's unavoidable. The loud noises could have been minimized if we were wearing our space suits and helmets," Mr. Guru explained.

While the spaceship continued orbiting around the Earth, the animal astronauts tried to peek out through the side window. They were spellbound by the magnificent view of the Earth. To their amazement, they could see the network of roads and streets on the Earth's surface.

From time to time the three animals found their excitement overshadowed with the anxiety of unknown dangers to come, but they were calmed by the presence of Mr. Guru, who looked pretty cool and relaxed. Mr. Guru was busy photographing the Earth from different angles. Suddenly, Finny broke the silence with a frightened cry,

"Loo...look! Gho...gho...Ghost!" stuttered the frightened Finny, pointing towards a pair of eyeglasses floating in mid-air around the cabin.

"They...they...look like my...my Grandma's glasses! I mean, when she was alive! I...I...feel her presence! I feel a chill! Grandma, is that you? Oh, no, I think I'm going to faint!" Happa cried out hysterically.

"I think...I think, it's an invisible space creature with glasses. He's going to destroy us and stop our mission," whispered Chalu nervously in Happa's ear.

Mr. Guru smiled. "That is a feature of **zero-gravity**. We'll encounter this often as we travel through outer space."

"What feature?" The animals shouted in unison, their eyes popping out of their heads.

"What kind of creature feature is this?" asked the panic-stricken crow, Chalu. "Mr. Guru, you say these creatures are plentiful in space? Oh, no! What will we do? They are going to attack us, devour us! We'll all die!" His voice cracked towards the end.

"Settle down, fellows! Don't overreact," Mr. Guru said smiling, thinking the animals were joking around. "To add to your fun, I'll make my pen fly!"

With these words, Mr. Guru let go of his pen and it started floating in mid-air, bouncing off of everything and anything it touched inside the capsule.

"Magnificent act, Mr. Guru! You are a terrific magician, I must admit," Finny shouted, feeling relieved. "Why didn't you tell us you were putting on a magic show in the first place?"

"This is no magic show, nor am I a magician. Any of you can make things fly here in space. These are normal events in zero-gravity environments! You're kidding me, right? You all know about **gravity**, don't you?" asked Mr. Guru, a bit perturbed.

"No, Mr. Guru. We don't understand any of this," said Finny.

"It is true! It is true! We don't understand it!" Happa and Chalu echoed.

"Goodness gracious!" Mr. Guru was shocked by their reply. "Didn't you have any lessons or training prior to this mission?" Mr. Guru asked anxiously.

"Sure Mr. Guru, we were trained well for our trip to the moon," Finny said enthusiastically. "First, we exercised every day to build up our muscles! We learned all about nutrition and were given strict orders not to consume any food or beverages on the moon. You can never tell what kind of mysterious germs you might catch which can cause strange illness. Then, we learned German, French, Chinese, Arabic, and even the ancient languages like Latin and Sanskrit to communicate with the moon beings. Since we're not sure what language they speak on the moon, we've mastered sign language too! We invented it ourselves. It's like this; we open our mouths and point at our stomach when we're hungry and close our eyes and say, 'zzz...' when we're sleepy. I think we've discovered an universal language! It's bound to work!"

"Besides all that," Finny continued, "we've learned to be gentle and polite to the moon beings. We were told to keep smiling and to speak sweetly to win their hearts. In case of an enemy attack, we've been trained in judo and karate. We don't believe in using dangerous weapons like knives or guns for self-defense. If it fails, we've also mastered the act of playing dead. This is really an easy one to learn. All you have to do is lie down on the ground without moving or breathing and pretend to be dead and..."

"Stop it! Stop it right this second!" Mr. Guru said. He was terribly upset. "I've got a clear picture of your *outstanding* astronaut training. Outstanding in the sense, that it's so incredibly awful that it stands out like a sore thumb. I've never heard of such a thing!" Mr. Guru continued, "What luck! Why me? Why do I have to be stuck with the 'Three Stooges' of astronauts on an important space mission like this?" Mr. Guru continued in a regretful voice. "How can I have a successful moon mission when you don't even know the ABC's of space travel? This is an extremely disturbing situation."

Mr. Guru looked very disturbed and he sat silently for several moments, lost in thought. Finny, Happa and Chalu felt humiliated by Mr. Guru's outburst. They felt uneasy over Mr. Guru's prolonged silence, but they didn't know what to do about it. So, they sat in their seats quietly, like a guilty party awaiting the punishment. Finally, Mr. Guru looked up at the animals' gloomy, serious faces and broke the silence.

"Please forgive me for carrying on like that. I hope I haven't offended you. I didn't mean to blame you. This whole situation is entirely my fault. I should have realized the woods would be an inadequate setting for space training even though Mr. Vim assured me to take care of the astronaut training. I should have realized that Mr. Vim couldn't possibly have known the types of training given to astronauts. He didn't even inform me about what was going on as far as your training was concerned. I should've taken measures from the very beginning to make sure you were trained properly," Mr. Guru continued.

"There's no use crying over spilled milk, though. We have to make the best of things. As far as I can see, we have two choices. We can simply forget the whole thing and go back home, or we can keep going and try our best. Of course, there are plenty of risks involved in this second choice, but with proper judgment and strong determination, things may work out."

"We choose the second! We want to keep going, even if it's going to be dangerous and risky," the animal astronauts cried enthusiastically.

"In that case, I'll need you to cooperate with me. I will be your teacher and instructor in this space mission and you all must listen, learn, and follow my directions very carefully. You must ask my permission before doing *anything*. Do you agree to this? If not, speak up! It's now or never!" Mr. Guru said.

"Agreed!" said all three animal astronauts.

"Good!" said Mr. Guru. "To start with, I'd like to give you a short account of the astronaut training that takes place at NASA before the space flights. The astronauts' training period lasts abut two years. During that period, they're briefed about space and space flights and are shown photographs and movies of all preceding missions. Then they are trained to survive and function under freezing cold and extreme heat in order to cope with the conditions they might encounter in space. The astronauts practice manning spacecraft in flight simulators at Johnson space center, NASA's headquarters near Houston, Texas. They're also strapped inside a big ball of a huge machine called a **centrifuge** which whirls them around at a high speed to accustom them to the speed and pressure they'll encounter during spaceflight. In order to simulate a weightless environment, the astronauts practice working long hours underwater. They also practice working inside special planes which simulate a weightless environment by making rapid dives from high altitudes.

"Now, I'll explain the mystery of the floating eyeglasses and pen. Be attentive and ask questions if you don't understand it, because asking questions is one of the best ways to learn," Mr. Guru continued.

"Gravity is a force which pulls everything towards it like a magnet pulling the metals towards its surface. Gravity exists within each and every object, starting from the tiniest particle to a huge mountain. Things attract each other by this force. The bigger the object, the stronger the pull of gravity. Our Earth has a powerful gravitational force that pulls everything down towards its center and keeps everything in the right place. It keeps the water in the ocean, the air in the sky and our feet on the ground. Without this force everything would float around in space.

"Because of the gravitational pull of the Earth, anything you toss up in the air is bound to fall back to the ground. To escape the pull of gravity, we need to travel at a super fast speed called an **escape velocity**, which is approximately 25,000 miles per hour. Going any slower, we wouldn't be able to escape the Earth's gravity completely.

"You must have noticed how Apollo 11 and our spacecraft went up in three different rocket stages to break loose from the Earth's gravity. The first-stage rocket of Apollo 11 had a fuel tank of 22 tons of liquid oxygen and kerosene. When the fuel was ignited, this rocket lifted the heavyweight Apollo 11 to a height of 38 miles in the air at a speed of 6,000 miles per hour. After a couple of minutes, the exhausted fuel tank separated from the spacecraft and fell into the ocean. The **escape tower** jettisoned itself into space."

The Spaceship goes up in 3 different stages

"What is an escape tower?" asked Happa.

"The escape tower is an emergency launch escape device. It is a tower-like structure with a small rocket that's attached to the tip of the spaceship. The astronauts can escape with this if an emergency arises during or after the first few minutes of the launch," Mr. Guru explained.

"I was wondering why didn't the spacecraft take off at escape velocity, 25,000 miles per hour, from the very beginning?" Finny asked.

"Good question!" said Mr. Guru. "It's much more convenient and safe for a spacecraft and its crew to accelerate gradually from a low to a high speed, because there are many risk factors involved in starting with a very high speed. The most important among them are, stress on the structure of the spacecraft and tolerance of the astronaut's body to high pressure. Remember the tremendous pressure you all felt during the take off of our spacecraft? We could hardly breathe! Well, imagine how you would have felt if our spacecraft would have taken off with a speed of 25,000 miles per hour! It would have been life threatening! Moreover, a spacecraft taking off at full speed can easily catch on fire from the friction with the Earth's atmosphere.

"Have you noticed fast-moving bright streaks of light in the night sky that disappear almost as soon as you see them? These are called *shooting stars* or *falling stars*. In reality, they're not stars at all, but **meteors**. A meteor is a small body of stone or metal. They catch on fire from the friction caused by entering the Earth's atmosphere. Most of the meteors burn down before they reach the ground, but a few survive and land on Earth. These are called **meteorites**. To avoid becoming a shooting star, Apollo 11 and our spacecraft as well went up in three different rocket stages. A powerful multistage **Saturn V rocket** was used for launching the cone-shaped Apollo 11 in three different stages with three different speeds," Mr. Guru explained.

"What is a rocket, Mr. Guru, and how does it work?" Happa asked enthusiastically.

"A rocket is a booster which provides a thrust to the spacecraft to go forward. It's a big cylinder or a tube with an opening or nozzle at one end. The cylinder is filled with chemical fuel, which is stored either in dry or liquid form. When this fuel is ignited, hot gas forms, expands, and gushes out through the cylinder's nozzle. The force that's created when this gas is released pushes the spacecraft forward. Have you ever noticed what happens when you let all of the air out of a balloon through its nozzle? As the air from inside the balloon rushes out through the nozzle, the balloon flies fast in the opposite direction. It's the same principle with a rocket."

"The second-stage rocket contained liquid oxygen and liquid hydrogen fuel. When this rocket was ignited, it accelerated the speed of the spacecraft (15,000 miles per hour) and lifted Apollo 11 spacecraft to a higher altitude of about 114 miles and put it in an orbital path called, Earth Orbit. This orbital path is also known as the **parking orbit**, because it's like a parking place for the spacecrafts. At this altitude, the spaceships can stay up here and orbit around the Earth without any effort, with its rocket engine shut off. After that second burn, the second empty fuel tank was also detached from the spacecraft and dropped down to Earth."

"Mr. Guru," Chalu cried out. "You mentioned about an orbital path. Where is it? I don't see any kind of path around here? It's all empty space!"

"An orbital path isn't a real visible path or a road of some kind. Planets and stars orbit along an imaginary curved path known as an orbital path. There are two main types of orbital paths: circular and elliptical (oval). To travel along a certain orbital path, a spacecraft must reach a certain speed. The speed of a spacecraft is calculated by scientists according to its distance from the Earth. In this case, Earth orbit is an imaginary path at this altitude with an orbital velocity of 17,000 miles per hour," Mr. Guru explained.

"Anyway, the last engine was fired to give the spacecraft a third push into space. This third fuel tank contains liquid oxygen and liquid hydrogen fuel. It is the smallest one, because of the comparatively light-weight of the spacecraft. The third rocket boosted the speed (17,000 miles per hour) of Apollo 11 to an altitude of 115 miles and put it in a nearly circular orbit. The third booster was shut off after a few minutes, and remained attached to the spacecraft. Our spacecraft, 'Puspaka,' was launched the same way as Apollo 11.

"While completing one and a half orbits, the human astronauts and we have sufficient time to make a final check of all the operational systems of the spacecraft. If for some reason the astronauts decide to return to the Earth, it is easier to do so from this orbit. On the other hand, if everything checks out okay, the third fuel tank will be re-ignited again to put the spacecraft in an elliptical path and then accelerate the speed of the spacecraft (about 25,000 miles per hour). This final acceleration is called **trans-lunar injection**, and will allow us to escape the Earth's gravity completely. After this final maneuver, our spaceship will be propelled in the right track towards the moon," Mr. Guru continued explaining.

"You should all know a bit about the originator of this idea of gravity and his interesting way of discovering it. The idea of gravity was pioneered by a famous scientist named **Newton**."

"Newton!" Happa cried out, interrupting Mr. Guru. "I know all about him!"

"Bravo Happa! I'm delighted that at least one of you knows about Newton's discovery," Mr. Guru praised Happa. "I'd be happy to have you tell the story of Newton's discovery to your friends."

"Thank you, Mr. Guru. I'd love to," Happa started enthusiastically. "One day, Newton was sitting beneath an apple tree close to a pond and eating a piece of apple pie when suddenly, an apple fell from the tree, landed 'plop' right on his head, and then rolled down onto the ground. 'Ouch!' Newton cried. 'It's strange,' he mused. 'When the apple is made into a pie, it's so soft and so delicious, but it's so hard and painful when it hits you on the head!'

"Newton had a sore bump on his head for a while, and then he applied an herbal paste made out of garlic and turmeric. Like magic, the paste soothed his pain and levelled the bump, I mean cured the bump on his head."

'Grandpa Newton' Story

"Well, which one of these two is Newton's famous discovery? The 'two faces' of the apple— in other words, the soft and hard properties of the apple, or the pain killing, bump removing herbal paste?" Finny asked with a sly, mischievous grin.

"Neither!" Happa snapped. "Why don't you keep quiet and listen! I haven't come to his famous discovery yet," Happa seemed irritated.

"Yes, please continue, Happa," Mr. Guru said.

"Thank you, I will. "As I was saying, this incident made Newton wonder why the apple didn't fly up into the air or fall into the pond. Why did the apple fall to the ground, right next to him instead? Newton was convinced that there was a reason behind this. He sat there thinking for hours, staring at the apple and smelling it, scratching it and nibbling on it. Then, suddenly he flung his hands up in the air and jumped up and down with joy shouting, 'Praise the lord! Hallelujah! By Jove, I've got it! The Almighty Lord wanted to offer this delicious fruit to his best Earthly creations, the land creatures, like the humans and the rabbits! He didn't intend this fruit to be eaten by the airborne creatures like the crow or the water creatures like the fish!' These are the great thoughts that popped up in my Grandpa Newton's head," Happa finished her story with an expression of pride and satisfaction.

Both Chalu and Finny were burning with anger at Happa's story but kept their emotions contained and awaited Mr. Guru's opinion. Mr. Guru cleared his throat, looked at Happa and said,

"Happa, your story described the wishful thinking of a rabbit instead of any discovery of a scientist. I didn't expect you to narrate your Grandpa Newton's great ideas, but the great ideas of a human scientist by the name of **Sir Isaac Newton**. He pioneered the concept of gravity. I think I'd better tell the story. When Newton saw the apple fall to the ground, he began to think that the Earth might have a hidden force, which he called gravity. He discovered that this force pervades the entire universe. The sun's gravity holds the Earth and all the other planets in our solar system in their places. His theory of the *'Universal Law of Gravitation'* and the *'Theory of Motion'* are the most significant contributions to the field of astronomy.

"Now, let's get back to our discussion of why these objects like my eyeglasses and the pen are floating around the space capsule. I'll try to explain it to you in the simplest way I know," Mr. Guru continued. "At this point, our spaceship is more than one hundred miles above the Earth and the Earth's gravity extends up here in space too. Our spaceship is literally in a kind of constant fall around the curve of the Earth. The spacecraft and everything inside are also falling at the same rate and at the same speed. So, we're all in a free fall."

"Oh, no! Mr. Guru, if our spaceship is constantly falling around the curve of the Earth, then eventually it'll crash and we'll be history!" Finny said anxiously.

"It is not the kind of fall you're thinking of," said Mr. Guru. "Our spacecraft is never actually going to fall to the Earth because the speed of our spaceship and the Earth's gravitational pull are in balance. As long as our spacecraft keeps going at this speed, we'll stay in orbit and we won't be pulled down to the Earth. For example, take a piece of stone and tie it securely to the end of a string. Then hold the other end of the string and swing it high above your head in a continuous circular motion. You'll find that the stone will stay up as long as you continue swinging it around, even though the Earth's gravitational force is pulling it down. The moment you stop swinging, the stone will fall back to the ground.

"Our spaceship is like that piece of stone and the gravity is like the string. The spaceship is staying up because it's traveling in a circular path around the Earth with a constant speed. The force which keeps the spinning object away from its center is known as the **centrifugal force**. Even though the Earth's gravity exists up here in space, we don't feel it inside the spacecraft when we're traveling at a constant high speed. It feels like a zero-gravity (no gravity) environment and we feel weightless. Zero-gravity— 'zero-g' for short, is also called **micro-gravity** by scientists.

"Weightlessness and zero-gravity result from the balance between the gravitational pull of the Earth and the inertia or the motion of the spacecraft. These objects, like my eyeglasses or the pen are floating here, inside the cabin, because they are weightless. If we were not strapped to our seats, we would also be floating like the glasses or the pen in a weightless state," Mr. Guru explained.

"How does it feel to be weightless, Mr. Guru?" Happa asked.

"The feeling of weightlessness is like the sensation of the sudden plunge on a roller coaster or a sudden stop in an elevator. On Earth, this feeling is temporary. This sensation goes away as soon as things become normal. In space, this feeling continues as long as you are in orbit. It's a kind of slow-motion state with a strange and relaxing feeling. Unbuckle your seat belts, and you will see what I mean!" said Mr. Guru.

The animals undid their seat belts as Mr. Guru asked. As they did, they began to float around the cabin. They bumped into each other and into the walls, shouting, "Ouch! Oops!" and "Wow!" They giggled and laughed and pointed at each other. Then they began performing all kinds of difficult acrobatic tricks— triple flips and backward somersaults— just like circus performers. Finny the fish picked up Happa the rabbit with the thin tip of his tiniest fin. It was easy, because the animals were completely weightless without gravity.

"Look at me, fellows!" shouted Finny in a excited voice. "I am the greatest weight lifter ever born under the sun! Man! Lifting heavy objects up here is a cinch!" Finny laughed.

Soon, however, they began to feel sick. Their heads were aching and their stomachs were churning and they started throwing up. Mr. Guru, who was watching from his chair, helped them back to their seats and gave them water to drink. After a while, the animals were back to normal, but they weren't too eager to undo their seat belts again.

"A zero-gravity environment creates many obstacles for the astronauts in their activities," Mr. Guru started. "As you can see, our shoes also have magnetic soles that keep us from floating inside the spacecraft. There are hand coils and hand rails attached to the ceiling and walls, and foot restraints attached to the module's floor. This is so we astronauts can move around easily inside the capsule. Our meals are also specially prepared for a zero-gravity environment," Mr. Guru explained.

"Right now, I am deciding to change our scheduled time for the trans-lunar injection. I would like to delay it a bit and put our spaceship at a higher altitude to orbit around the Earth."

"What for?" asked all three animals simultaneously.

"Because, I want you to have a very special experience and see a unique sight at that orbit! Trust me, this delay will not make much difference in our arrival time on the moon."

"Then, Let's go for it!" shouted the animals in excitement.

Mr. Guru fired the rocket and increased the speed of their spaceship to go to a higher orbit.

Chapter 4

A Space Walk

"All right, astronauts," Mr. Guru said. "I think it's time for you to see a little bit of outer space, and I know a great way for you to start your exploration. Why don't you all go for a 'space walk?' This is a very special experience— you put on your space suits and float around outside the capsule. The human astronauts first tried this back in 1960 during the Gemini 4 spaceflight and repeated it several times during the Gemini missions. The first man to perform a 'space walk' was a Russian cosmonaut (astronaut) named Alexei Leonov. The first American to do a 'space walk' was astronaut Edward White. Now's your chance to be the first animal astronauts to go for a 'space walk.' Our capsule is fully equipped for extravehicular activities, or EVA for short. I'm sure none of you would want to miss out on this rare opportunity.

The fish, the rabbit, and the crow exchanged doubtful looks, for none of them really wanted to venture outside of the capsule to perform the 'space walk.' They were all very quiet until, finally, Chalu spoke,

"I admit that I enjoy flying. I also enjoyed floating inside the capsule— except for the side effects, that is. I suppose it would be fun to fly in the wide open sky without using my wings, but Mr. Guru, I can't bear the thought of going outside and performing a 'space walk!' Think of all the things that could happen out there in the wide open space! What if I float far away? That would be the end of me for sure! And that miserable sick feeling after a 'space walk'— oh, I can't bear to think about it. Not to mention all the space creatures we might encounter. Who knows what we're going to run into out there? The whole idea scares the pants off of me, Mr. Guru. It really does!"

"Come on!" Mr. Guru said. "Don't let a little headache or a stomachache ruin your adventure. You had what's known as space malaise or Space Adaptation Syndrome. That shouldn't keep you from having a little fun and adventure! In any case, these sicknesses don't endanger your life in anyway! Our spaceship is well stocked with medical supplies and I know how to treat the symptoms. Besides these temporary conditions like headaches, dizziness and nausea, I also have remedies for more serious space illnesses that are caused by living in a zero-gravity environment over a long period of time. Those are; weight loss, puffing up of the face and limbs, weakening of leg muscles, loss of bone calcium, change in the blood pressure and circulation, and changes in various chemicals in the blood stream."

"How do the astronauts catch these illnesses?" Happa asked.

"Well, our bodies are designed to function under Earth's gravitational pressure," Mr. Guru started. "In a zero-gravity environment, the body functions change. First of all, our bodies no longer weigh anything. Second of all, without gravity, there is no up or down. As you might have noticed, our spacecraft is traveling upside down, but we don't feel it. Normally, our hearts have to pump very hard against the force of gravity to circulate blood to the upper parts of our bodies. But in a zero-gravity environment, our hearts slow down because they don't have to pump so hard to send blood to the upper parts of our bodies. So, all the fluids in our bodies start to circulate more freely and we end up with more fluid than normal in our arms, faces, and heads. As a result, we start to look puffy and flushed. The muscles in our legs become weak because we haven't been using them. All of these things make us lose our appetites and we start to lose weight," explained Mr. Guru.

"There is one good thing about a prolonged stay in zero-gravity, though. Astronauts usually grow a couple inches taller in space. This is because the vertebrae in the spine don't stay compressed like they do on Earth. Without gravity, they begin to stretch out, making us astronauts a couple of inches taller. Some astronauts have even been known to outgrow their space suits! Anyway, you don't have to worry about these long-term illnesses. I promise you'll have a safe and delightful 'space walk,' if you stick to my instructions. So.o.o... who's going to be the first volunteer?" Mr. Guru asked.

Chalu was convinced. He raised his wing in the air and shouted, "I will! I will!"

"Very good, Chalu. Don't you two want to get in on the action?" Mr. Guru asked, turning to Finny and Happa. Neither one had any interest in taking a 'space walk,' so each one tried to push the other forward.

Mr. Guru turned to Finny and said, "You should have been the first to volunteer for the job. A considerable amount of astronaut training is spent

The fish jumped into a crater, but there was no water. (see page 44)

The rabbit could jump six times higher on the moon. (see page 47)

underwater, because the water simulates the zero-gravity effect. As an underwater creature, you're more used to weightlessness than us land-dwellers. Be a sport and join in. This is a once-in-a-lifetime opportunity. You don't want to miss out on this, do you?"

"You have my full support, Mr. Guru," Happa said. "Yes sir! You sure picked the right candidate, a perfect partner for Chalu. Even though it's called a 'space walk,' it's really floating in space. As I see it, floating in space and swimming in water are basically the same. I think a perfect swimmer like Finny would be a great space walker. Unfortunately, I, being a four-footed animal, am totally unfit for the job. I haven't got the slightest idea how to fly or swim!"

Finny scowled and said, "You sure have a way of recommending others in order to save your own neck, Happa! But don't forget, it is called 'space walk,' not 'space float!' Men invented it and they have only two feet. I'm sure if a two-footed man could go for a 'space walk,' a four-footed rabbit like you could do an even better job. You're really a much better candidate than I."

Mr. Guru could wait no longer. He said, "Time is running out. You've all had your say. Now listen to me. Don't be chicken and shy away from a good challenge! Have a positive attitude and some self-confidence— trust me, it will take you a long way down the road of life."

Finally, he convinced the three animals to go for a 'space walk.' Chalu, Happa, and Finny started putting on their bulky, white space suits, special helmets, and padded gloves under the supervision of Mr. Guru. The space garments were cumbersome and they could hardly move.

"Mr. Guru!" Chalu complained. "Do we have to put on these silly outfits just to go for a walk? I prefer to fly light. Moreover, all the space suits are the same color, silvery white! It is not my favorite color, you know! Why don't they make colorful space suits?"

"Sorry, but you have to put on those garments! These will be your lifesavers in space or in any other hostile environments like this," Mr. Guru said.

"What's so hostile about empty space?" Chalu asked, surprised. "I don't see anything dangerous around here!"

"Of course you don't!" said Mr. Guru with a smile. "Almost all of the hazards are invisible to the naked eye! First of all, space is a vacuum, meaning it is empty. There is no air, no atmosphere, no pressure, no anything. This vacuum will kill you in an instant, if you are exposed to it," Mr. Guru explained. "The extreme hot and cold temperatures existing up in space range from 250^0 Fahrenheit in the sun and minus 150^0 in shadow and that will burn or freeze unprotected astronauts to death. Space is also filled with harmful radiation which destroy the body tissues of living things, causing death. Besides these invisible dangers, there are tons of flying objects like large and micro meteorites that might collide and could cause serious injuries leading to disability or death. So, to protect you from all these calamities, your space suits are indispensable!

"These bulky space suits are specially designed for astronauts like ourselves, by technical experts who take many factors into account concerning the safety and comfort of the astronauts. I'll tell you an interesting story about a costume designer for NASA who was in charge of designing space suits for the astronauts. While designing, he wanted to add flexibility to these bulky one-piece space suits so that the astronauts could move and function freely. He thought it over for a while, but couldn't come up with a solution.

"One day, he was having tea outside in the garden when he noticed a caterpillar crawling up a branch. The caterpillar was folding his body in bunches and then stretching out to move forward. Suddenly, the designer got an idea for his space suit— he'd copy the movement of the caterpillar. He went back and added bunched up folds to the arms and legs and other parts of the space suits and designed them accordingly."

"Isn't it amazing that a tiny caterpillar could open the eyes of an expert in designing a space suit?" Happa said excitedly.

"Yes! Very often, insignificant small events give rise to significant discoveries," Mr. Guru said. "The idea of flying came from watching birds in flight. **Louis Pasteur** discovered airborne bacteria while trying to help farmers stop their beer and wine from going sour. The steam engine was invented by **James Watt** after he watched the intense pressure of steam in a covered pot of boiling water.

"In any case, when dressing, the astronaut has to put on undergarments before putting on the space suit. The undergarments are equipped with special waste-disposal devices. The **space suit** is made with twenty-one layers of material to protect the astronaut from the vacuum state, flying debris, cosmic rays, and the extreme temperatures in space. The suits are made white in color and coated with silver because it reflects heat and keeps the astronauts cool.

"The **helmet** covers and protects the astronaut's head and face. A double-layered visor is built into the helmet. This visor is made out of special materials and tinted with gold to cut down on glare and provide clear vision. Two-way radios are fitted inside the helmets so the astronauts can communicate in space.

"The padded **gloves** cover the astronaut's hands and help with handling hot and cold materials during the 'space walk.' You'll need these for your 'space walk,'" Mr. Guru explained.

He handed each of the animals a **space gun** called **HHMU** (hand-held maneuvering unit), which has three nozzles and a compressed-oxygen gas tank.

"Using the pressure of the gun blast, you can turn in any direction you desire in outer space. If you shoot to the right, you'll move towards the left and vice versa, ands if you shoot to the front, you'll move backward," said Mr. Guru.

Then he attached the gold-coated **oxygen hoses** to the animals' space suits. These hoses were also connected to the ship's oxygen supply. He pressurized their suits by pumping oxygen into them.

Mr. Guru explained as he did this, saying, "Since there's no air in space and intense pressure as it's a vacuum, you need to remain attached to these oxygen hoses. These cords will supply you with oxygen to breathe and keep you at a comfortable body pressure. The oxygen hose is also known as **umbilical cord**, because it's just like an umbilical cord inside a mother's womb which provides a fetus with oxygen and other life sustaining facilities."

Mr. Guru attached small packs to their chests that contained a ten-minute supply of emergency oxygen. He explained, "These small packs of oxygen are for emergency use only, in case the oxygen hoses malfunction."

Lastly, Mr. Guru made sure that the 25-foot gold-coated **tethers** which were hooked to the spacecraft were secured, one to each animal, so that none of them could drift away into space. As a final measure, Mr. Guru slowly released all the oxygen in the capsule. By doing this, he created a vacuum just like that in space, which would allow the animals to exit the ship without difficulty. Then he opened the hatch of the spacecraft and asked the animal astronauts to walk out.

First, Chalu climbed out of the spacecraft carefully, followed by Happa and Finny. He tried to take his first step out with caution, and the other two astronauts did the same, but it was useless— all three floated around aimlessly and slowly drifted further and further away from the spaceship.

"Ooooo! What a strange sensation!" The three animals exclaimed. It gave them goose pimples all over their bodies. Chalu spotted an object with a long, arm-like thing sticking out of it— floating higher up in space.

"Hey fellows! What's that up there?" Chalu asked through the intercom inside his space suit, while drifting further away.

"What's what?" the other two animals shouted, as they struggled to stop drifting by moving their wings and legs.

"That thing with the long arm!" Chalu shouted, as he pointed out the object to his two friends. "Looks like some kind of space creature to me!" Chalu said nervously.

The other two animals became equally nervous at the sight of the strange floating object. In a rush, they all shot their oxygen guns and tried to head back toward the spaceship, but in their haste, they went on shooting like crazy in all directions. Their guns ran out of oxygen and they couldn't get near the spacecraft. In fact, they kept drifting and drifting until all of a sudden they stopped and felt the tethers tug them back. They weren't drifting any longer, but they still couldn't figure out how to return to the capsule.

"Mr. Guru!" Chalu cried through his radio to the wise owl who was waiting in the capsule. "Save us! How do we get back to the spaceship? Our guns don't work anymore— they've run out of oxygen— and there's a space creature coming towards us with outstretched arms."

"Do something fast, Mr. Guru! Our lives are in danger! Hurry!" cried out Happa and Finny.

"Don't panic, fellows! Relax and listen to me carefully," consoled Mr. Guru. "There is no creature or any such thing out here in space. I see the floating object you're talking about. It's probably a *satellite* and it's in a higher orbit."

"What's a satellite?" Chalu asked.

"A satellite is an object circling around another object in space. The moon is a satellite of the Earth, because it orbits around the Earth. At this point, our spaceship is considered a satellite of the Earth, too, because it's orbiting around the Earth now. Our spaceship is an artificial satellite, whereas the moon is a natural satellite of the Earth.

"There are thousands of man-made satellites orbiting the Earth at different heights. Some of them are communications satellites for television broadcasting and radio and telephone transmission. Others are weather satellites that monitor weather patterns on Earth. There are also space satellites out here that study distant stars and galaxies and military satellites that spy on military units in foreign countries. So don't worry! Grab your tethers, hold on tight, and try to pull yourselves back to the capsule. It's not easy, but you'll do just fine," said Mr. Guru.

The animal astronauts caught hold of their tethers and tried to get closer to the spacecraft, but they floated off in every direction *but* toward the ship. Finally, with a lot of difficulty, they pulled themselves back alongside the spacecraft. They thanked the wise owl and tried to do their 'space walk,' moving along next to the spacecraft with the help of their tethers. All the animals were spellbound by the radiant blue glow of the Earth against the background of deep, dark space. The animal astronauts were floating in space more than one hundred miles above the Earth. They could still see the outlines of different continents against the deep blue oceans.

"Wow! What a heavenly sight!" Chalu proclaimed. "I've never seen such a spectacular earthscape in my life, not even from the tallest tree or the highest mountain!"

After a few minutes, Mr. Guru instructed the three space walkers to get back inside the spacecraft. The animals quickly returned to the craft. Mr. Guru closed the door of the capsule until it was tightly sealed. He then re-pressurized the cabin by filling it with oxygen. The three animals and the wise owl settled down comfortably after taking off their heavy space suits. All of a sudden, the bright sunlight faded away and night approached. The animals were perplexed by the short duration of daytime, but they didn't say anything, thinking that perhaps they'd lost track of the time during their 'space walk.'

Chalu started yawning, and thought he'd settle in for a good night's sleep. "Good night, friends! Good night, Mr. Guru! I'm retiring for the night. I'm used to hitting the sack by sundown. It's an old habit." With these words, Chalu began looking for a bedroom.

"Mr. Guru!" Chalu cried upon finding the bedroom. "There are no sleeping arrangements in here! Where are the beds? For that purpose, a leafy branch would have suited me just fine! But how am I going to sleep now?"

"Sorry, Chalu, there are no regular beds in here. There is no room or need for them up here! You just get inside one of the sleeping bags hanging from the wall and go to sleep. You'll be just fine! You may look like a hanging bag of crow, but you won't feel any difference whatsoever, because in a zero-gravity environment, one feels quite normal in any position. Make sure to strap yourself into the sleeping bag; otherwise, you'll float around," Mr. Guru explained.

Chalu got inside a sleeping bag, strapped himself in, and tried to sleep. A few minutes later, the sun rose and bright sunlight flooded the cabin.

"Good heavens!" Chalu said, looking out of his sleeping bag in surprise. "No! It can't be! It can't be daytime so soon! I'm either dreaming or losing my mind! This 'space walk' has affected me badly, I think!" Chalu looked very disturbed as he got out of his sleeping bag and floated slowly towards Mr. Guru.

"Mr. Guru," Chalu complained. "I think that the 'space walk' has messed up my nervous system! My sense of time is gone. I am going mad for sure. One minute it was night-time, and the next minute it was day again. I'm so confused!"

Mr. Guru chuckled, much to the other animals' bewilderment.

"This isn't funny, Mr. Guru! We feel the same way as our friend, Chalu. We must be suffering from the same kind of nervous disorder. The 'space walk' has cast an evil spell on us. We're going crazy!" Happa and Finny complained.

"No such thing has happened to you, my friends! You're all perfectly fine," Mr. Guru said, still chuckling. "Short day and night *are* really happening here in this orbit. Our spaceship is now in an orbit where the cycle of day and night is only 90 minutes— 45 minutes of day and 45 minutes of night. We're circling the Earth faster than the Earth's rotation around its axis, which means that there'll be more than one sunrise and sunset during each Earth day. Just watch the **terminator**, which is the dividing line between the illuminated and the dark side of Earth. The sunrise and the sunsets near the terminator are heavenly sights, I must say!" Mr. Guru paused.

The animals witnessed sunrise and sunset every 90 minutes and passed through day and night cycles every 45 minutes. It was shocking for the animals to see day and night approach so suddenly. They witnessed the most beautiful and unique sunrise when their spaceship entered the daylight side of the Earth. The first light of the sun appeared as a faint light-curve around the Earth's horizon and then suddenly swelled up into radiant bands of blue and red colors. Then these dazzling colors disappeared in a few moments, followed by the sudden appearance of the glaring sun. After 45 minutes, the animals saw the multiple-colors reappeared near the horizon before their spaceship plunged into the enveloping darkness of the sunless side of the Earth. They were surprised to see lightning flashes in the deep darkness of the night side. The lightning was flashing, one bolt after another, inside huge storm clouds which were there next to each other and making them light up like giant light bulbs.

"Wow! What a wonder! How beautiful!" thought the animals.

"Now," announced Mr. Guru, "we're ready for the trans-lunar injection. I will re-ignite the third-stage rocket to get away completely from Earth's gravity and head towards the moon. So all of you get ready and buckle up."

With these words, Mr. Guru pressed a button and re-ignited the rocket. The engine fired, boosting the moon-bound spacecraft to a speed of 25,000 miles per hour. The spaceship of the animals headed towards the moon.

Chapter 5

≡Off to the Moon

The animals settled into a daily routine of doing housekeeping chores, such as: cleaning up the inside of the module, chlorinating and recycling the water supply, recharging batteries, and checking fuel and oxygen reserves as well as grooming themselves, eating, resting, and listening to music. They also took several photographs of the Earth and the moon.

Their meals were bite-sized, and either dehydrated or freeze-dried, which meant that all the water had been removed from the food. Before they could actually eat their meals, they had to add water to the food with a special gun. They drank water or juice either with straws or by squeezing the plastic containers inside their mouths. Every time the liquids spilled, they floated around the capsule like tiny balloons and the solid foods that escaped were floating like blobs. The animals had fun chasing after the balls of liquid or blobs of solid.

"Hey Chalu," said Finny. "Please catch my ball of drink, which is floating next to you. It just escaped my mouth. I would like to have a sip with my straw!"

"I caught it!" said Chalu. "But Finny! Your drink-ball has split into many droplets! You should be happy now, because you can have several sips instead of one!"

"Boys! Please don't mess with that floating blob down there!" said Happa. "That's my AGSM!"

"Do you mean, that floating blob is your Awesome Gourmet Space Meal—AGSM for short?" asked Chalu jokingly.

"No!" said Happa smiling. "In this case, AGSM stands for Awful Gushy Space Mush!"

After a while, the animals' fun died out. They were getting tired of their food. It was pretty messy!

"Gosh, Mr. Guru," Happa complained. "These space meals are no fun! They taste so yucky. It feels like eating toothpaste from a tube! I wish we could've brought our snacks with us!" She sighed.

Mr. Guru smiled. "Yes, I agree with you. This food has no flavor, but that's not just because of the way it's prepared. It's also partially due to us. You see, we can't really smell the food, and our sense of smell effects our sense of taste. We can't smell because in a 'micro' gravity environment, more blood rushes toward the upper parts of the body. This causes the blood vessels inside the nose to swell and gives you a stuffed-up nose, just like when you have a cold. Regular food would probably still taste better than these meals, but there's not enough room in the capsule to store all the provisions we'd need. These bite-sized meals are just the right size for our tiny kitchen. Besides, it's messy and dangerous to eat regular food up here in this zero-gravity environment. The food and crumbs would fly all over the place and soon we'd have trouble breathing or seeing. There's hope for our next mission, though, because I've heard that soon they'll be making a new kind of space meal for us astronauts that's much tastier than these and much more convenient to eat."

As the spacecraft headed for the moon, the animal astronauts got tired of waiting for night to come. They couldn't figure out why there was still daylight flooding the capsule. The sun seemed to be stationed in one spot and shining away.

"Now what's wrong?" Chalu asked. "How come the sun isn't setting? I'm tired! What should we do, Mr. Guru?"

"You are witnessing the true form of the sun," explained Mr. Guru. "The sun is always shining in space. It doesn't rise or set like we see on Earth. Day and night are created by the Earth's rotation around its axis or the motion of the spacecraft around the Earth. Let me explain it to you," Mr. Guru continued. "The Earth rotates around its axis from the west to the east, so we see the sun rising in the east and setting in the west. The side of the Earth facing the sun has daylight, while the opposite side is dark. In the process of rotation, the night side of the Earth slowly turns towards the sun and becomes lighted and the previous lighted side becomes dark. Right now, we're so far from the Earth that it can't cast its shadow on our spaceship to create night. It's three-day journey to the moon, and we won't have a minute of darkness the whole time. However, if you pull down the window shades, you should be able to sleep comfortably."

"How strange! Either we face a very short day and a very short night, or we face a never-ending day! Isn't there any place up here where there's a 24 hour day and night cycle like there is on Earth?" Chalu asked out of curiosity.

"Sure there is!" answered Mr. Guru. "Scientists call it **Geostationary** or **Geosynchronous Orbit**. This orbit is at the height of 22,300 miles above the Earth's equator with an orbital velocity of 6,900 miles per hour. NASA has put many communication satellites in that orbit for the convenience of telephone transmission, radio broadcasting, and TV broadcasting. This orbital period is exactly the same as the rotation of the Earth. At this orbit, satellites will hover motionless at a fixed point over the Earth. So, under those conditions, the day and night cycle is 24 hours. However, at that orbit, you're usually not in the shadow of the Earth and it's still light out all the time."

"Shoot!" Chalu shouted in disappointment. "That spoils the charm of the geostationary orbit for me! It may be fine for those communication satellites to hang up there, but for a tired, sleepy crow like me who's looking for a long dark night, it just won't do."

When the spacecraft got within 30,000 miles from the moon's surface, the gravity of the moon started pulling the spaceship away from the Earth's gravity. Their spacecraft started speeding up as it headed toward the moon. It got closer and closer and the moon became larger and larger. Soon the **craters** on the surface of the moon became clearly visible.

Finny the fish was overjoyed to see thousands of big and small craters. He thought, "Boy, oh boy! I sure am going to love this place! Man, this is heaven! I've never seen so many swimming pools in one place! I can swim away my time! Ah, that cool, refreshing dip, that tingling feeling— I can feel it already. What fun!"

Happa couldn't believe she was actually looking at the surface of the moon from up close, and that soon she'd be landing on it, too! The distant moon that she used to watch from Earth always seemed like a dream world to her. She loved the soft and silvery touch of the moonlight because it was so soothing and relaxing for her body and mind. She was especially excited over the idea of meeting her favorite storybook characters, 'the moon god' and his 'pet rabbit.'

"Oooo...how lucky I am, to be landing on the moon! I sure will try my hardest to find and meet the 'moon god' and his 'pet rabbit' I heard about in a story. Oh! How splendid the 'moon god's' palace must be! It must be built out of gold and silver, decorated with emeralds, rubies, and diamonds. If I do find the 'moon god,' it will be like my dream come true," Happa continued dreaming.

Chalu stared fixedly at the moon's approaching surface. "Wow!" he thought, "a wide open space. How wonderful! As soon as the spacecraft touches the moon's surface, I'm going to jump out and fly away. I'll go round and round in circles till I drop down, dead tired. As long as I'm on the moon, I won't think of anything other than flying. That's a promise to myself!"

In the meantime, Mr. Guru was busy observing and taking pictures of the moon's surface. Minutes passed in silence until Mr. Guru's voice disturbed the animals' daydreams.

"May I have your attention?" Mr. Guru spoke. The three animals became attentive.

"It's time for us to make a crucial decision. Apollo 11, the main spaceship of the human astronauts, is named **Columbia**. It's an assembly of three separate sections.

3 Sections of Apollo 11

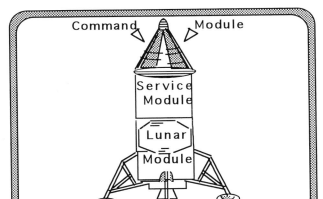

"The cone-shaped first section is called the **command module** (CM), which contains the control center and carries the astronauts. The command module is the only part of the spacecraft designed to return to the Earth.

"The second part is the **service module** (SM), which is like a storeroom. It holds the spacecraft's main rocket, fuel, and other supplies like oxygen, water, and electric power stored in dry battery cells.

"The last module is the **lunar module** (LM), Code-named **Eagle**. Eagle is the national bird of the United States. The lunar module is also nicknamed **Spider**, because it resembles a spider with its long legs. This module is designed to land on the moon's surface and return back to space.

"Pretty soon, we'll be firing our **retro-rockets**, which will slow our spaceship and put it in an orbit around the moon. Retro-rockets in a spaceship act like breaks in a car or train and also help change direction in the vacuum of space," Mr. Guru explained. "Then, our spaceship will descend 70 miles above the moon's surface and orbit the moon in a circular path. From this height, the human astronauts will deploy the lunar module and descend down toward the moon with two of the astronauts, Neil Armstrong and Edwin Aldrin, inside. Michael Collins will pilot the **CSM** (the combined unit of command module and service module) as it orbits the moon.

"After the lunar exploration is over, the lunar module will leave the moon's surface with these two astronauts and rejoin the command module in space. Then, Neil Armstrong and Edwin Aldrin will return to the command module and eject the lunar module into lunar orbit. Then, they'll eject the service module into space just before returning to Earth in the command module." Mr. Guru paused for a couple of seconds and then started speaking again.

"Our spaceship is a smaller version of Apollo 11. It has three similar sections. We have to follow the same procedures as the human astronauts to land on the moon. We can't land on the moon with all three parts of the spacecraft intact, because it is not designed that way. Even if somehow or other we managed to land on the moon in the whole spacecraft, lifting off from there would be difficult, because of the heavy weight.

"Right now, our problem is finding a pilot. None of you have the technical knowledge or training to pilot a spacecraft. I am trained to pilot the craft, but if I stay behind in the command module, you three won't be able to operate the lunar module. There's no other choice— I *have* to join you in the lunar module and land it on the moon. We're going to have to leave the command module in this orbit without a pilot inside. When we return from our moon exploration, we won't be able to get back home, because the lunar module is too flimsy to re-enter the Earth's atmosphere," Mr. Guru paused. "However, if we get lucky, we might be able to catch up with the command module in this orbit when we return from the moon. If not, our last resource is to contact NASA and ask them to rescue us. As I see it, once we've come this far, we may as well take the chance and go all the way. What do you say to that?" Mr. Guru looked up at the animals for their response.

"Let's go! Let's go!" they started shouting.

"So be it; let's go!" the wise owl said enthusiastically.

Mr. Guru fired the retro-rockets to slow the spacecraft down and put it in orbit around the moon. After that, he maneuvered it to descend and positioned it 70 miles above the moon's surface in a circular orbit.

"Now, let me open the hatch that leads to the lunar module. You all follow me and crawl through the tunnel into the lunar module," said Mr. Guru.

The animals followed Mr. Guru. Once they were inside the lunar module, Mr. Guru shut the hatch door and made sure it was tightly sealed. The space inside the lunar module was limited. It was barely big enough for the four of them to stand up. Mr. Guru fired the engine and the lunar module separated from the command module.

After firing the retro-rockets again, the lunar module began its direct descent, making its way down toward the moon, its legs facing upward. As it neared the surface of the moon, Mr. Guru fired the retro-rockets to slow it down further. The module had descended from an orbit of 70 miles above the moon to 5,000 feet above the moon. Now the spaceship's computer took over the descending procedures and maneuvered the module perfectly. At the precise, planned moment, the retro-rocket was fired and it flipped the lunar module back to its upright position, legs facing downward. For the first time, the animals had a close-up view of the lunar surface through the module's triangular windows. The lunar module now descended towards the moon very, very slowly— slower than the falling of a dry leaf in autumn.

Chapter 7

On the Moon

Finally, the module carrying the animals touched down on lunar soil, gently blowing the moon dust from the ground. The landing was smooth and perfect. The engine was turned off. For a moment, there was silence inside the spacecraft. The three animals and Mr. Guru peered anxiously through the module's window. Countless big and small stones were scattered all over the place. The land seemed to be covered with a black and white powdery dust. There were craters everywhere. Many big craters and literally thousands of small craters covered the ground. The landscape ranged from ashen gray to shiny white with huge boulders, rolling hills and high mountain ranges in the distance.

"Mr. Guru, I can't see the Apollo 11 spacecraft or any of the human astronauts around here! They must have landed on the moon by now!" said Finny anxiously.

"Yeah! Where are they? We don't see even one of them!" asked Chalu and Happa simultaneously.

"The Apollo 11 astronauts must have landed their Lunar module on the moon, in an area called the **Sea of Tranquillity** and we have landed our lunar module in an area called the **Sea of Rainbows**. The Sea of Tranquillity is pretty far from this place! We can't go there to greet them or anything but we can talk to them by two-way radios. In the subsequent Apollo missions, the astronauts will have electrically propelled **lunar roving vehicles** or '**moonbuggies**' for their transportation on the lunar surface," said Mr. Guru.

"In any case, I just talked to the human astronauts by my two-way radio. Apollo 11 astronauts landed on the moon on **July 20**, at the Sea of Tranquillity. The landing was not easy for them, because the lunar module was about to land on a crater about the size of a football field covered with large rocks. Astronaut Neil Armstrong took over the manual control and steered the spacecraft to a smoother spot to land.

"After landing, Armstrong immediately sent a radio massage to the

Mission Control: *The Eagle has landed.*' The very first words uttered by astronaut Neil Armstrong as he stepped onto the moon were *'That's one small step for a man, one giant leap for mankind.'* He is absolutely right!" said Mr. Guru smiling. "The most interesting part is, Richard Nixon, the president of the United States spoke to the astronauts on the moon by telephone from the Oval room at the White House. He congratulated them on their success. Anyway, we are the first animals on the moon!" Mr. Guru declared merrily.

The fish, the rabbit and the crow cheered, crying out, "Long live the animals!"

"Let's get out of the module fast and start exploring," Chalu said excitedly.

"Not so fast! We have to prepare ourselves first. I'll explain and you do as I say," said Mr. Guru. He instructed the animal astronauts to put on their space suits, helmets, and life-support systems. While Mr. Guru, Finny, and Happa were busily getting ready, Chalu was becoming impatient to get out of the module. He yawned and stretched his wings lazily, thinking,

"Oh my! My poor wings feel like they're paralyzed from sitting cramped up in this small spaceship. Now, I'll fly a couple of laps across the moon, and get some exercise. I'll sneak out and be back in here with the others before they even realize it. Who needs all those gadgets here on the moon, especially for such a short flight?"

Chalu slowly opened the hatch of the lunar module a bit to squeeze through the opening when suddenly he was sucked out and all of the air from inside of the module rushed outside.

"Whew! What was that ?" Finny and Happa shouted out in a panic.

"Oh no! The module door is opened a bit! We're being sucked outside by the air as it escapes from inside the module. Luckily we have our space suits on already. Where is Chalu?" asked Mr. Guru in a concerned voice. He and the other two animal astronauts started looking around for Chalu.

In the meantime, Chalu flapped his wings up and down fast, attempting to fly. But alas, he fell. He fell to the ground like a lump of rock. He felt like he was choking. He couldn't breathe, and his lungs felt like bursting! The blazing rays of the sun felt like sharp arrows shooting into his body. He felt as if his blood was boiling and the veins under his skin were bursting open. He felt as if he were on fire.

"Help! Somebody help! Mr. Guru! Happa! Finny! Anybody! Please help me!" Chalu cried out in pain. To his amazement, he couldn't even hear his own voice. Still, he kept on shouting for help, hoping his friends would somehow hear him, but his efforts were in vain. None of the animals responded to his cries.

Fortunately, Finny spotted Chalu lying flat on the ground next to the module, his eyes closed, his wings outspread, and his beak hanging open. It seemed like Chalu was trying to say something. Finny notified everyone right away. Mr. Guru lowered the lunar module's ladder hurriedly and rushed out, carrying the crow's space suit, helmet, and life-support system. Mr. Guru and the other two animals picked Chalu up and quickly dressed him in the space suit and helmet, then attached the life-support system to his back. Chalu slowly regained consciousness. He opened his eyes a bit and looked up to see the concerned sad faces of his friends hanging over him. He felt bad that he'd caused such a catastrophe. Happa and Finny sighed in relief to see Chalu recovering. They smiled at him and tried to comfort him.

As soon as Chalu seemed out of danger, Mr. Guru started speaking,

"You are very lucky to be alive and well. Imagine what tragedy it would've been if Finny hadn't seen you at just the right moment. By now, we would be preparing a funeral for you." Mr. Guru seemed very upset and a little bit annoyed.

"I can't understand it!" muttered Chalu, still in shock. "How come an expert flyer like me couldn't fly on the moon? I'm a complete failure! I am an embarrassment to my fellow birds on Earth!"

"You must not feel that way, Chalu! Flights require air and the *moon is airless*. So, without air, one can't fly or breathe, as you might have realized by now," explained Mr. Guru. "The *moon has no atmosphere*. Without any atmospheric blanket, the sun rises over the lunar horizon and shines instantly with its full blaze. It continues to climb up in the lunar sky, maintaining its full strength until it sets. So on the moon, there is no dawn or twilight. The unfiltered sunlight reaches a temperature of 250^0 Fahrenheit and penetrates the skin like a razor. It will burn you up within seconds. Also, the moon is similar to the vacuum state in space. It can kill any living thing in a couple of seconds by bursting open blood vessels inside the body," Mr. Guru continued.

"On Earth, the sky looks blue because the atmosphere scatters the sunlight towards us. On the moon, in the absence of an atmosphere, the lunar sky

The rabbit lit a big fire and jumped into it (Folk-tale of India). (see page 52)

The churning of the "Milk Ocean" (Mythology of India). (see page 77)

looks black and one can see the sun and the stars at the same time," Mr. Guru explained. "Look up and you'll see for yourself!"

The three animals looked up and to their amazement, they saw the bewitching spectacle of the sun and the stars side by side against the black lunar sky.

"Why is it that there is no atmosphere on the moon, Mr. Guru?" asked Happa.

"One of the reasons is, the moon has very weak gravity and so it couldn't hold onto its atmosphere and slowly lost it into space," Mr. Guru said.

The animals spotted a blue and white half-circular ball rising over the lunar horizon.

"Look at that blue and white half-circular ball!" shouted Happa and Finny in surprise. "How strange! We didn't know that the moon has its own blue and white moon!"

"It looks much bigger and brighter than our moon though!" exclaimed Happa.

"That half-circular ball with a white and blue pattern is none other than our planet Earth! Most of the blue colored areas are the scattered sunlight and the white areas are the cloud patterns. Earth shines much more brightly during the lunar nights than the moon shines on the Earth," Mr. Guru explained, smiling.

"Our Earth! Wow! What a magnificent view! Earth-rise on the lunar sky! We'll treasure this view as long as we live," cried out Happa and Finny.

"Yes, it's a magnificent view!" said Mr. Guru.

"Long live planet Earth!" the animal astronauts cried.

Slowly, Chalu recovered from his shock and started speaking again with a sad look and a cracking voice.

"There's something bothering me that I have to talk to you about it. During my accident, I cried out for help and called you all by your names, but no one showed up or even responded to me! I feel like none of you really care about me. Is it too much to expect a bit of sympathy or help when you're in trouble? After all, we're partners in this mission. Did you all become deaf by some strange phenomena, or did you just pretend not to hear me? Right now, you all seem to hear me perfectly well! I really cannot understand this. Could someone explain it to me?"

Mr. Guru laughed out loud and said, "You need not be so upset, my friend! We certainly do care for you. Be sure of that! In this case, no one could be blamed. The truth is that on the moon everyone is deaf because the moon is airless. Air acts as a carrier for sound. When sound is produced, it creates vibrations or waves in the air, like ripples on the water of a pond when disturbed. The sound waves travel until they reach the eardrum. As a result, we hear sounds. Here on the moon, the sound waves cannot travel because there is no air. So, we need special devices for hearing and conversing up here. Inside our space suits and helmet we have oxygen and two-way radios for communication so we can talk and hear each other. You snuck out without the necessary gadgets. As a result, we could not hear your cry for help and you suffered the consequences.

"These space suits, helmets, boots and life-support systems are vital to keep astronauts alive and comfortable in any hostile environment like space or this moon. Our space clothing is designed to protect us from extreme conditions on the moon, like the intense heat of the lunar day, which soars to a temperature of 250^0 Fahrenheit and the teeth-chattering bitter cold of the lunar night, when the temperature falls down to 200^0 below zero. It also maintains our body pressure at a normal level. Each of the life-support units on your back is packed with devices essential for your survival in this hostile environment. Inside the life-support system, there is oxygen for breathing, a regulator to maintain body temperature, a communication radio, and water that circulates through the space suit and keeps you cool. You can also drink this water by sipping from the tubes in which it's transported," Mr. Guru concluded.

Soon after Mr. Guru finished his talk, Finny announced, "Well, I'm feeling kind of dry and I've had burning sensations all over my body for the past few days. So, you all continue your interesting discussion while I take off for a quick dip in a nearby crater. See you later, fellows!"

Before anyone could say another word, Finny headed off in the direction of a small crater. He paid no attention to Mr. Guru's warning cry— "Stop! Don't do it! There is no water inside these craters!"

Seconds later, Finny reached the crater. He closed his eyes and jumped in, but there was no water. "Oh, well, the blazing sun must have evaporated the little water it contained," he thought. "No big deal. There are tons of pools around here! I'll go swim in that big pool over there."

He ran over to the nearest big crater he saw. He looked down inside, but it was too dark for him to see anything. "The water must be down there at the bottom," thought Finny. He took a deep breath and did a front flip into the crater.

"Ouch...Ouch...Ooouch!" Finny cried in pain. "This is horrible! There is no water in here! Where did it all go? Oh, God! My bones are broken into pieces. I am crippled. Lord, have mercy on a little fish like me! Save me!"

By this time, Mr. Guru, Happa, and Chalu had reached the crater's rim and were peering inside.

"Ahoy, down there! Can you hear me? Are you all right?" Mr. Guru called.

"Are you asking me, Mr. Guru?" Finny asked in a pained voice. "You must be joking! How can I be okay? I'm broken into bits and pieces like shattered glass! Oh...oh...oh...I hurt so much! It's a miracle I'm still alive! I hear death knocking at my door. Good-bye pals! It's been nice traveling with you." Finny's voice trailed off.

Mr. Guru, trying to comfort him, said, "Calm down, Finny. We'll try to rescue you from the crater. I explained many times before that you must not do anything without my permission. But you were stubborn and foolish, and so you invited this trouble. I don't know how I ever thought this mission would be smooth sailing in the first place!"

"How can we sail without water, Mr. Guru?" Finny cried out from the crater, misunderstanding what Mr. Guru had said. "How is it that these pools on the moon are so dry? Doesn't it rain here on the moon, ever?"

Even in this serious situation, Mr. Guru could not help but laugh at Finny's child-like question. "Yes, you're so right Finny," Mr. Guru continued. "*The moon surface is waterless*. These bowl-shaped holes or ditches on the moon are not pools. These are called craters and they are void of water, because there's no atmosphere. A planet requires an atmosphere containing water vapor in order for it to rain. No atmosphere means no rain, and no rain, no water. These craters were created by millions of meteorites that bombarded the moon's surface in its early history. Some of these craters are products of the moon's internal volcanic activity.

"You can see various kinds of craters on the surface of the moon. Some have central mountain peaks. The largest craters are surrounded by rugged mountain ranges whose peaks measure as high as 3 miles. The craters with bright white lines surrounding them are known as **rayed craters**, which are relatively young. There are craters filled to the brim with lava that seeped up from the moon's interior when meteorites struck the surface.

"The dark plains you see are called **maria**. Mare means "sea" in Latin and maria is plural of mare. These were once the largest craters created by the bombardment of meteorites. But later, lava covered up those craters and cooled down to form these large areas of maria. The largest maria measures up to 625 miles across."

"Boy! It must be awfully loud here on the moon with those meteorites falling all the time!" said Happa.

"Here on the moon, the meteorites fall completely intact without any sound because of the absence of atmosphere and air," explained Mr. Guru.

"Please...oh please, Mr. Guru," pleaded Finny from the bottom of the crater, "lift me up fast! If a big meteorite falls on top of my crater, I'll be buried alive. Even small meteorites could crush the rest of my broken bones into lunar dust. Or, if a volcanic eruption starts, I'll be grilled— a grilled fish! How awful! Oh, no! I can't talk about this any longer! I'm too young to die, Mr. Guru! Don't let this crater be my grave! Instead of being known as the first live fish on the moon, I'll be remembered as the first dead fish on the moon. On top of that, I'll have to roam the huge lunar surface, a lonely ghost!" Finny continued moaning as he spoke.

"Don't worry, Finny! We'll get you out in no time," comforted Mr. Guru.

Happa and Chalu tried to calm Finny down by cracking jokes and telling funny stories. Mr. Guru asked Happa to go back to the lunar module and bring out the rope that he had brought along in case of an emergency. Happa quickly hopped back to the lunar module and returned moments later with the rope. Mr. Guru tied a knot shaped like a loop at one end of the rope and lowered it down into the crater. He told Finny to slip the loop around his waist and tighten it. Then, he had Happa and Chalu's help to pull the rope back up with Finny on it. Finally, a very weary Finny emerged from the crater.

"Thank goodness that crater wasn't very deep," Mr. Guru said. "Otherwise, our rope wouldn't have reached the bottom. If that crater had been any deeper, I don't think we would've been able to save you."

Mr. Guru began to examine Finny by touching and pressing different parts of his body. He was relieved to find nothing more than a few minor bruises.

"You weren't injured very badly, Finny, partly because you were wearing a thick space suit, and partly because the gravitational pull is weaker here than on Earth. If you had fallen into a ditch of this depth on Earth, you would have been broken into pieces, even with your space suit. This is because the Earth's gravitational pull is much stronger, and so your fall would have been much harder," said Mr. Guru.

"Let's get out of here fast, Mr. Guru!" Finny said as he stood up with a bounce. "As you explained earlier, the meteorites fall here on the moon without a sound. What will happen to us if a big meteorite fell here right now? We might not even have time to say our prayers. Let's hurry back and keep our eyes peeled for falling meteorites."

"But, Finny," Chalu cried. "What if we fall into a big crater while walking with our eyes fixed on the sky?" Mr. Guru and Happa burst out laughing at Chalu's comment.

"Hey guys, listen to my discovery," Happa announced.

"Oh, no! Not another one of your Grandpa Newton stories!" Chalu said.

"This is my own genuine discovery and quite a significant one at that," Happa continued. "When I went back to the lunar module to fetch the rope, I tried to hurry up by hopping higher and faster. Guess what I discovered, guys?"

"What did you discover?" cried Chalu and Finny at the same time.

"I found that I can jump much higher here than I can on Earth! See for yourselves! I'll prove it!" With these words, Happa started jumping higher and higher shouting, "Hey, down there! Check it out! Look at my super high jump!"

It seemed like Happa had a pair of springs for her feet. She jumped several feet higher above the heads of the animals. Finny and Chalu kept on watching with amazement.

"Bravo! Bravo! Keep it up, Happa!" Chalu and Finny cheered. "You are going to be famous on Earth! People will start calling you 'Super Rabbit' with this new talent of yours! You will be the unbeatable champion in basket-ball!"

Mr. Guru smiled and said, "Your hopping talents will go back to normal the moment you set foot on the Earth, Happa. The reason you can jump so high on the moon has to do with gravity. As I mentioned before, the moon's gravity is weaker than the Earth's— it is *one-sixth* of the Earth's gravity. So

Happa can jump six times higher here than on Earth. Our body weight is also an outcome of gravitational pull. If Happa weighs sixty pounds on Earth, she'll only weigh ten pounds on the moon. As you can see, we had very little difficulty in moving around with our bulky space suits and carrying our large backpacks, because they weigh one-sixth of their weight on Earth. A human astronaut's space suit with the backpack weighs about 200 pounds on Earth," Mr. Guru concluded.

"Come on, all of you!" Happa invited. "Join me in a super-hop. It's a lot of fun, I say!"

Chalu and Mr. Guru decided to give it a try. Both agreed that hopping on the moon was really fun. Finny sat quietly watching his friends hop around like Mexican jumping beans. His friends tried to persuade him to join in the fun, but Finny decided not to since he was still sore from his fall inside the crater. After a while, the jumpers got tired out. Happa looked around for a shady place to rest.

"Looking for a tree or a bit of shade perhaps?" Chalu teased. "Well, friend, let me give you a piece of advice. Forget the tree. It is too much to expect around here. There isn't even a blade of grass on this rugged, barren land! When I fell down earlier, I looked all over for a tree or bush to land on, but all I found were piles of stones, heaps of sand, and those darn craters."

"Why, even if the moon's surface is like a desert, desert-type plants could grow here, such as cactuses and desert shrubs! Isn't that true, Mr. Guru?" Happa asked.

"It's not true," Mr. Guru said. "In the absence of water, air, and proper soil, there is *no plant life on the moon*. As a matter of fact, there is *no life form* of any kind on this land. If you wish to rest, come inside the lunar module with me. Afterwards, we will all come out and continue our exploration."

Happa wanted to spend a little more time outside the lunar module. She tried to convince Mr. Guru by saying, "Actually, we're not that tired, Mr. Guru! We don't need to rest. The three of us would like to stay out here a few minutes longer. It's not very often that one gets an opportunity to spend an afternoon on the moon. Don't you agree, Chalu and Finny?"

Chalu and Finny nodded their heads in agreement, even though they were exhausted. Mr. Guru told them to stay close to the lunar module and not to try any funny business while he went into the capsule to take a rest.

Chapter 8

The Picnic

All three animals sat outside and tried to think of something fun to do, but they couldn't really come up with anything. Minutes passed. Finally, Chalu spoke up.

"Let's see who can throw the most stones into the craters."

"That's dumb," Happa said.

"Why don't we play hide-and-seek?" Chalu suggested.

"Nah. That's a little kids' game. We're too old for that," Happa said.

"Well, I don't understand you, Happa! It was your great idea to have fun outdoors! But you don't seem to be interested in anything I have suggested so far!" said Chalu. "There is nothing else we could do around here to have fun! How about listening to some space-age poems? I've been inspired by the moonscape and have composed some creative masterpieces while sitting out here. Are any of you in the mood to hear them?"

"Sure, sure! By all means, start! We would love to hear your recital," Finny said, for he was bored to death.

"Thanks," Chalu said. "I wish I had my guitar to play while singing! But of course, we wouldn't be able to hear the music since there is no air on the moon. In any case, you might have heard my first piece before, as it is the space-age version of an old nursery rhyme." He cleared his throat loudly and started singing.

> '*Jack and Jill went up to the moon*
> *to fetch a pail of water.*
> *Jack and Jill looked far and near*
> *But all they found — dry craters.*
> *Stones up here and hills down there*
> *dry and barren land.*
> *That made Jack mad and Jill so sad*
> *They went back hand in hand.*'

"Wonderful! Delightful!" cheered Finny, while Happa sat quietly without saying anything.

"The next one is for all the friends and happy couples on the moon, created by me, Chalu, after a famous romantic verse," said Chalu.

> ' Here beneath the black lunar sky.
> The sun and the stars are shining high.
> We, inside the silvery suits.
> Sipping water from the tubes.
> We will jump and hop around, like the Kangaroos.
> We will sing through intercoms, like the birds, cuckoos.
> You and me together...Wow!
> This wilderness, a paradise now!'

"Superb! How modern! How romantic!" Finny shouted, clapping his fins. Happa remained silent and aloof.

"My pleasure," replied Chalu. "The moon isn't really the wasteland it seems. Besides providing inspiration to artists like me, it can be an ideal place for practicing yoga. Yoga or meditation is very good for your health, you know! Also, it can be an ideal spot for picnics and games."

"Did you say picnic?" Happa jumped out of her seat and stood up. "Picnic! Hurrah! What a great idea, Chalu! You're a genius to think up such a brilliant idea, and of course your space-verses were sheer genius, too. Now we'll have some real fun! A picnic on the moon! If we don't have enough food for a big picnic, at least we can still have a cozy tea party. Nothing warms me up like a steaming cup of tea. What do you say, fellows?"

"Sounds great!" said Finny and Chalu, who were getting bored.

"Let's get busy," Happa said excitedly. "You two gather a few medium-sized rocks and build a fireplace. In the meantime, I'll go back to the module and fetch tea, a pot of water, and some scrap paper to light a fire. "Happa departed for the capsule, hopping and humming a merry tune along the way.

Finny and Chalu collected several moon rocks and built a fireplace. Meanwhile, Happa returned with the picnic supplies. She placed a covered pot of water on top of the fireplace and stuffed scrap paper under it. Then she pulled out a book of matches.

"Good heavens!" Finny exclaimed with a smile. "You brought matches to the moon!"

"Oh, yes! I always travel with two things," said Happa. "A small compass which was a very special gift from my grandma and my 'energy box,' as I call my book of matches. I found this matchbox in the jungle. I think of these two objects as a rabbit's best friends. By lighting a fire with my matchbox, I can cook my meals if I want, keep myself warm on cold winter nights, and scare off my enemies. I also use it to find my way in the dark. The compass needle shows the direction in which I am traveling. But for some strange reason, the compass is malfunctioning here on the moon! Anyway, I also have a very special reason to carry this matchbox. I'm saving the last match to light for the moon god."

"Moon god?" cried Finny and Chalu simultaneously. "Who is he?"

"Well, he is my hero! My destiny! He is a character in a story I heard when I was young," Happa paused.

"Tell us the story. We'd like to know about him, too. Besides, we love to hear stories," Chalu said enthusiastically.

"Yes! Please tell us," Finny said excitedly.

"All right then, I'll begin," Happa said.

"Once there lived a rabbit in a jungle. He had a great fascination for the moon. He adored the moon and worshipped him as his god. On moonlit nights, the rabbit would sit on a hilltop and gaze at the moon for hours with undivided attention. Then he would sigh and say, 'Oh, how I wish to live on the moon forever!'

One day, the rabbit decided to perform a special worship to show his sincere devotion towards the moon god. The rituals he performed were very rigorous! The rabbit would have to fast without food or drink from sunrise till sunset. It's like a hunger strike to get your wish. Then, after sunset, he would worship and pray to the moon god and serve a big meal to whoever showed up at his door. After the guest was fed, the rabbit would break his fast for the day. If no guests showed up, the rabbit would keep fasting till the next evening.

Days passed by. One time for a week or more, no guests came to the rabbit's door. But, the rabbit continued his fast. He became weaker with each passing day, but still he didn't give up his fast.

Then, the night of the full moon finally came. The big, bright moon appeared in the sky pouring down silvery moonshine all over the jungle. The rabbit's heart throbbed with joy and excitement at the sight of it. He climbed up to the top of a hill and kept watching and praying to the moon as it progressed higher and higher in the sky. Suddenly, the rabbit was startled by a voice coming from behind him. He turned back and found a man in rags standing in the moonlight.

'I am very hungry and tired,' said the beggar. 'I haven't eaten for days. I traveled a long distance to come here to you after hearing of your kind hospitality towards your guests. Please give me something quick to eat.'

The rabbit was overjoyed to have a guest after so many days. He offered the man a seat and asked him to sit down and rest while he brought him some food. The rabbit tried to find some food for his guest, but his cupboards were bare. It was late at night and he was too weak to go out and find anything. So, he went back to his guest and stood in front of him with folded paws and addressed him politely,

'O honorable guest, I consider myself very fortunate to have you as my guest. It's my duty to serve and satisfy you to the best of my ability. At this moment, I have nothing better to offer you than my own body. Please accept it as your meal to satisfy your hunger. In a few minutes, I'll be cooked over the fire and ready to eat.'

With these words, the rabbit gathered a few dry twigs and leaves from the ground, lit a big fire and jumped into it. What a wonder! The fire didn't burn the rabbit or touch even a single fur of his coat. The rabbit was bewildered. He looked for his guest, but to his amazement he found not the beggar, but a divine figure dressed in exquisite clothes and jewels.

'I am the moon god,' the divine figure said, smiling at the rabbit. 'I have come down from heaven disguised as a beggar to test your devotion and determination in pursuit of me. You proved yourself more than worthy to get your wish. I am very pleased with you. So, I grant you your life's ambition, to live with me forever. This story of your devotion and sacrifice will be remembered by all living things

for years to come. Come along, I will take you with me.' With these words, the moon god picked up the rabbit from the fire, patted him gently, held him close to his heart, and vanished.

"From that day on, we've been able to see an imprint of the rabbit on the moon. So you see, if the 'moon god' decides to appear and test me to see if I could be his second pet rabbit, I'll have my matches ready to light a fire and jump inside," Happa concluded.

"Lovely story," praised Finny and Chalu.

"Well, Happa, you've come this far. Now all you have to do is find your 'moon god,'" said Chalu.

"Right this minute, the matches will be useful to light the fire for our tea party," said Happa, as she tried to light the match. One, two, three. She tried many times, disposed of several match sticks, but still she couldn't light even a single one.

"How strange!" mumbled Happa. "These matches aren't even sparking!"

"Give it to me," Chalu said, as he snatched the matchbox from Happa. "I can do a better job than that." Then Chalu tried lighting the matches. Same story. There wasn't a single spark.

"Hand it over to me! You fellows don't know the trick of lighting a match, but I do! I've got the magic touch," said Finny, as he grabbed the matchbox and tried in vain to light one. All three animals carried on with their match-lighting competition. They struck the matches on the surface of rocks, the bottom of their boots, the tops of their helmets and everything else they could think of.

Mr. Guru noticed this match-lighting commotion through the lunar-module window. He came down and asked the animals what was wrong. The three animal astronauts explained the situation and asked Mr. Guru to help them light the fire.

"Mr. Guru, please give us a new matchbox or show us some other way to light a fire for our tea party," begged Happa.

"Oh, no! No one can light a match or any kind of fire here on the surface of the moon! There's no oxygen on the moon. Oxygen is an element in the air and fire needs oxygen to burn. Without it, there's no way to light a fire. You can see for yourself by conducting a simple experiment on Earth when you return. Light a candle and then cover it up with a glass tumbler. You'll find that the lit candle will go out in a short while. This is because the oxygen quickly runs out inside the glass tumbler. Because of the moon's airless condition, our lunar module has a tank of oxygen in liquid form to ignite the engine and lift our module from the lunar surface when we take off.

Candle Experiment

This is fun!

"Anyway, there is no need to light a fire to boil water when the sun would do the job. I am sure that by now your water has not only boiled, but completely evaporated," Mr. Guru concluded.

Mr. Guru was right. The animals found their pot empty and hot.

"Mr. Guru!" asked Finny. "My compass needle doesn't show north and south on the moon like it did on Earth. What's wrong?"

"There is nothing wrong with your compass!" said Mr. Guru, smiling. "A compass needle is a piece of magnet. The two ends of a magnet are called poles. A magnet has a south pole and north pole. If there are two magnets, the unlike poles (north and south) of these two magnets will attract each other. Our Earth is like a huge piece of magnet. The needle of a compass points north and south on Earth because it is attracted by the Earth's magnetic poles. The moon does not have magnetism and so your compass is not showing any direction."

"What a waste of effort and energy," sighed Finny. "What an impossible place this moon is! I cannot understand why we had to race men to get to this barren, airless, waterless lifeless place first. There must be a thousand and one better places in space that we could have visited. I think we should have visited the sun which is so bright and glorious, instead of this dead world. Wouldn't you say so, Mr. Guru?" Finny looked at Mr. Guru for his opinion.

"You're right about the moon as far as its general form is concerned," said Mr. Guru. "The moon is a barren, dead world. But it is not a waste of effort, for, humanity's success in this moon mission will be the first step toward interplanetary travel.

"Men decided to explore the moon first because it is our closest neighbor in space. The moon is 240,000 miles from Earth. Men acquired plenty of information regarding the moon by using advanced telescopes and sending probes to the moon, such as the **Ranger**, **Lunar Orbiter** and **Surveyor** probes. The last of the surveyors was equipped with 1100 pounds of equipment. It soft-landed on the moon and successfully collected plenty of data about the moon's surface, structure, gravity, atmospheric condition, and many other things. Men used these informations to build spaceships, train astronauts, and eventually land on the moon. From this manned lunar expedition, the humans will acquire firsthand information about the moon that will be used to plan future space exploration. Apollo project will continue for several years and more human astronauts will come up here to the moon and collect scientific data which will allow scientists to learn more about the moon," Mr. Guru explained.

"Men have always dreamed of exploring heaven. Their dreams have been fantasized in paintings and books for centuries. Many writers in the olden days wrote stories about traveling in space with the help of borrowed birds' wings. Writer, Jules Verne, in his book '*From Earth to the Moon* ' wrote about traveling to the moon with the blast of a cannon ball. H. G. Wells wrote space fantasies about traveling through space and time in '*Time Machine*' and '*War of the Worlds*.' Later, human's fantasy took a turn toward science.

"In 1903, the Russian scientist, **Konstantin Tsiolkovsky**, published his scientific work and laid out the principles of space travel. He suggested the use of multistage rockets and liquid fuel. A Hungarian scientist named **Herman Oberth** published his work on space travel and experimented with small solid-fuel rockets. At the same time, a scientist in America named **Robert Hutchings Goddard** carried out independent research on rockets. Finally, in 1926, he fired his first liquid-fuel rocket. He laid the foundation for the advancement and success of space travel.

"The first artificial satellite to orbit the Earth was called **Sputnik** 1 which was sent by Russia and **Explorer** 1 was the first successful U. S. satellite. The very first man who went to space and orbited the Earth was a Russian cosmonaut, named **Yuri Gagarin**. He went around the Earth once in a spacecraft named Vostok 1. The first American to orbit the Earth was astronaut **John H. Glenn**. He went around the Earth 3 times in a Mercury spacecraft called Friendship 7," Mr. Guru explained.

"As far as the other planets are concerned, those are extremely far away from Earth. Humans are in the process of sending probes to far-away planets in our solar system. You should know that scientists have already sent a space probe called the **Viking 1 lander** to Mars— the fourth planet from the sun. It will land and explore the Martian soil. The Viking 1 lander must have landed on Mars, the same day as Apollo 11 astronauts stepped onto the moon. I am positive that one day, humans will have the knowledge to explore those distant worlds.

"In the process of exploring space, humans will enrich the basic sciences. Sometime in the near future, they may colonize space, the moon, or even distant planets to solve the population problem on Earth. They may mine and extract resources from other celestial bodies. They may even meet and communicate with some advanced extraterrestrial beings and benefit beyond their wildest imagination. So, space science should be considered of utmost importance in this age," Mr. Guru explained.

"As far as stars are concerned, our sun is the nearest star to us. It is about 93 million miles away. The sun is eight light minutes away from the Earth, meaning that sunlight takes eight minutes to reach the Earth. The speed of light is 186,000 miles per second. The sun is super hot. It is also super large in size. The sun's diameter measures up to 860,000 miles. A million Earths can fit inside the sun.

"By mentioning a journey to the sun, Finny reminded me of a famous amateur astronomer, **William Herschel**, who was the first to discover Uranus, the seventh planet in the solar system. In an earlier attempt to give a general picture of the sun, he described the sun as a luminous planet, covered with thick clouds. He also wrote that the sun was inhabited by living things."

"Is that so?" asked Finny promptly. "That's great! If there are living things on the sun, that's all the more reason why we should pay a visit!"

"We all agree with Finny! Let's go there!" said Happa and Chalu excitedly.

"Wait a minute! I simply mentioned Herschel's early ideas about the sun, but that doesn't mean that he was right!" said Mr. Guru. "Be patient and listen! William Herschel was wrong in his conception of the sun as a luminous planet. Later on, by observing through telescopes located both on Earth and on satellites orbiting the sun, concluded that the sun consists mainly of gases like hydrogen, helium, and a few heavy elements, such as iron and uranium. The sun is not a planet but a star that produces its own light and energy. Besides visible light, there are other forms of radiation which are given off by the sun. These are: *gamma rays, X-rays, ultraviolet rays, infrared rays, microwaves,* and *radio waves.* In any case, the sun provides light and heat that's crucial to all living things on Earth. But some of this radiation (gamma rays, X-rays, ultraviolet rays) coming from the sun, is harmful to life of any kind if they are exposed to these for a long time.

The Sun's Radiation

"But Mr. Guru," Finny interrupted, "we can see the light which comes from our sun but we can't see the other forms of radiation which you just mentioned. How do scientists know that they exist if they can't see them?"

"Special telescopes are designed by scientists for observing those forms of radiation. The existence of some forms of radiation can be inferred through their activities even through you can't see them with the naked eye," Mr. Guru explained. "Gamma rays are very energetic photons (particles of light) which are used in medicine to treat some forms of cancer. X-rays are used in photographing bones and tissues of the body. Ultraviolet rays tan your skin at the beach and also are used in sunlamps to tan skin and to heal minor surgical wounds. Infrared rays are given off by stoves, heaters and other hot objects. Microwaves are used for communication and also in microwave ovens which cook our meals real fast. Radio waves carry radio and TV signals which enable people worldwide to enjoy radio and TV broadcasts.

"As yet, there's no technology to build a spaceship that could withstand the intense heat of the sun and still carry astronauts. But I will send you on a trip to the sun by hypnosis! I will hypnotize you all and put you inside an imaginary spaceship that will carry three of you on a journey to our nearest star, the sun! I will describe to you all I know about the sun and under hypnosis, all of you will feel you were actually there."

"Mr. Guru! You know hypnosis too?" cried out Chalu. "Wow! This is wonderful! It will be a great adventure for us! What are you waiting for? Hurry up and hypnotize us!"

"Yes! Please do it fast! We're all ready to start the voyage!" said Finny and Happa.

"All right, get ready! You are going on a voyage through the sun!" announced Mr. Guru. "All of you try to focus your eyes on my fingers and concentrate! I will count to ten and snap my fingers and you all will be hypnotized instantly. Under hypnosis, you'll still be able to ask questions and hear my answers."

Following Mr. Guru's instruction, the three animals focused their attention on his fingers and waited quietly. Mr. Guru started counting from one to ten. The moment he said the number ten, he snapped his fingers and the three animals closed their eyes and were instantly hypnotized.

Apollo 11 Moon Mission

Apollo 11 taking off from
Cape Kennedy, Florida (courtesy of NASA)

Apollo 11 astronauts—left to right: Neil Armstrong,
Michael Collins, Edwin Aldrin (courtesy of NASA)

Astronaut Edwin Aldrin stepping down
the ladder on the moon (courtesy of NASA)

An American flag was planted
on the moon (courtesy of NASA)

Space Exploration and Achievements of NASA

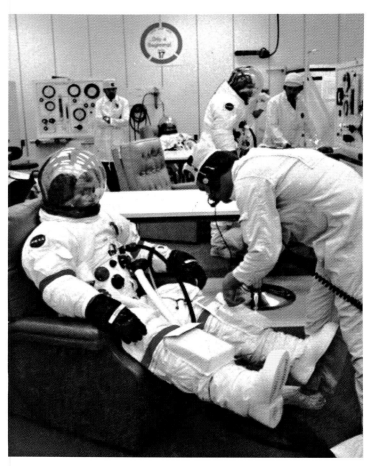

Astronauts' dressing room
(courtesy of NASA)

A lunar roving vehicle on the moon
(courtesy of NASA)

Control Room—The space flight center
in Houston, Texas (courtesy of NASA)

Astronaut Edward White performing
a "space walk" (courtesy of NASA)

Space Exploration and Achievements of NASA continued

Planet Earth photographed from space
(courtesy of NASA)

The Outer Layers of the Sun

The sun's corona (courtesy of NASA)

The Outer Layers of the Sun continued

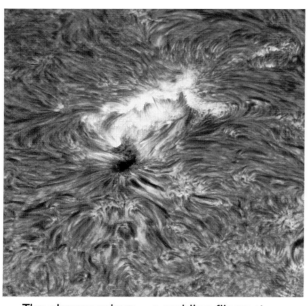

The chromosphere—a swirling filamentary
structure (courtesy Palomar Observatory)

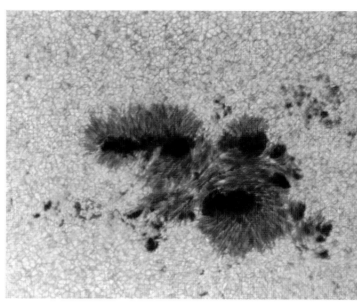

The photosphere—Solar granulation and sunspots
(courtesy Palomar Observatory)

Solar prominences (courtesy Palomar Observatory)

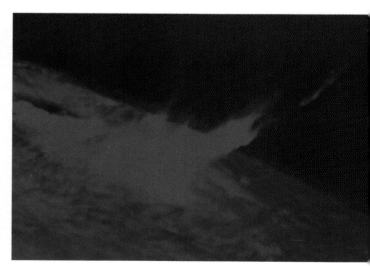

Solar flares (courtesy Palomar Observatory)

Chapter 9

≡A Magical Voyage through the Sun

"Now," said Mr. Guru, "you're all inside a spaceship heading toward the sun. Scientists divide the sun's atmosphere into three layers, even though there are no real boundaries between these layers. They are called: the Corona, the Chromosphere and the Photosphere. There is a very wide range of variation in the temperature inside these layers. Your ship's thermometer will read it.

The outer layers & the activities of of the Sun

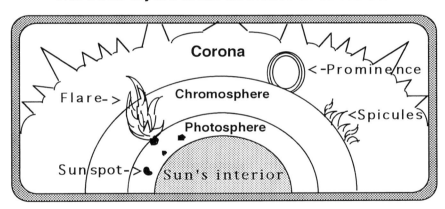

"The first layer or the outer layer of the sun's atmosphere you will travel is the corona (corona means "crown"). It is visible to us from Earth during a total solar eclipse (sol means "sun" in Latin). It appears as the bright halo crown around the sun. "

Happa, Finny, and Chalu found themselves inside a spaceship traveling toward the sun through a layer of atmosphere which was pretty thin and was made out of dust and gas. It looked bright and scattered, much like a full moon night on the Earth. It stretched for millions of miles in space. The animals couldn't see the end of it. The temperature was extremely high. The spaceship's thermometer read 36 million degrees Fahrenheit.

The spaceship continued its progress, when suddenly, it started shaking and rocking vehemently as if it was caught in a heavy storm. The animals peered out to see what was the matter. They found that a hot, gusty wind was blowing fiercely from the sun, carrying with it tiny glittering particles.

"Mr. Guru!" cried Finny, "the weather is pretty bad up here! We're in the middle of a violent windstorm and there are countless little glittering particles blowing through the sky!"

"You're traveling through the **solar wind**, which is a stream of charged particles, blowing out to space with the dust and gas from the sun," Mr. Guru said. "This wind blows at a very, very fast speed (900,000 miles per hour) and reaches out as far as the orbit of Pluto which is the farthest planet from our sun. The solar wind makes all the **comets**' tails swing back as they orbit the sun."

"Comets? Who are they? Comets have tails like me?" Happa asked in curiosity.

"Comets are frozen bodies of ice and dust. These ice balls melt and develop long shiny tails made out of dust and gas, when they orbit around the sun," explained Mr. Guru.

With the progress of the spaceship, the sun loomed larger and larger. The colossal size of the sun shocked the three animal astronauts. It was like an enormous ball of raging fire suspended in space! Huge flaming pieces of matter were flying out from the surface of the sun into space.

"Mr. Guru, what are we witnessing here? The bright and beautiful sun has suddenly turned into a monstrous ball of raging fire! It looks like it will engulf us totally! Look at all those flames! The sun is shooting out fiery flames all around space! We're going to be french-fried any minute now! Get us out of here!" Finny stuttered nervously.

"Don't worry, Finny. Just relax; you're perfectly safe inside the spaceship. The sun displays the most spectacular and never-ending fireworks. Keep watching— those fireworks are still to come," Mr. Guru explained.

The spaceship drew nearer to the sun. The animal astronauts saw huge, dark structures that looked like tunnels running through the sun's corona. They also heard a gushing sound coming from these tunnels.

"Hey, look! I've found the sun's sewage system! That must be the sound of the sewage gushing out," Happa said excitedly.

"Actually, what you're seeing are called **coronal holes**," explained Mr. Guru. "These dark structures are the magnetic tubes of the sun's atmosphere. These holes are the opening of magnetic tubes to the outside space. High-speed atomic particles blow out through these holes as the solar wind," he concluded.

The animals' spaceship slowly entered the next layer of the sun's atmosphere. The temperature in this layer was much lower than the corona. It was $50,000^0$ Fahrenheit. The entire region had a swirling, filamentary look. It was covered with huge fingers of glowing gas that resembled blades of grass.

"Wow! Look at that!" said Finny. "Mr. Guru, this area looks like a burning prairie or a burning grass field!"

"Those fiery spikes look more like long tongues of giant lizards to me! It's a whole field of flaming tongues, I must say!" Chalu cried.

"You have entered the second layer of the sun. This layer is thicker than the corona. It is called the chromosphere or color sphere (chromo means "color"). The chromosphere is invisible to us most of the time because the glare of the sun's bright surface hides it. Only during the solar eclipse, it becomes visible as a thin pink ring around the sun just before the totality," Mr Guru explained.

"Those flaming tongues or grass are actually strands of gas flames, "Mr. Guru said. "They're called **spicules** ("little Spikes"). They look like small blades of grass from a distance, but they're actually quite huge. A single spicule can measure up to 435 miles in width and 4,351 miles in height— almost 1,000 times higher than Mt Everest! The entire chromosphere is basically made out of these flaring spicules. The swirling pattern you see inside the chromosphere, is produced by the interaction between the hot gas and the sun's magnetic field. The sun has a very strong and complex magnetic field. Huge electrical currents run in its gases. You will see many fiery activities of the sun which are triggered by electrical currents within the sun's interior."

Suddenly, there was a tremendous explosion. Surges of gas flames streamed upwards, lighting the face of the corona. The three animal astronauts found themselves inside their spaceship, rising higher and higher above the sun's surface.

"Hey! What's happening?" shouted Finny as he looked around. "Oh, my God! Guru, our spaceship is being lifted up by a huge streamer of flaming gas that shot out from an explosion! We are sitting on top of the flame!"

"What should we do now? How do we get down to the sun's surface!" screamed the three animals.

"Don't worry! You will come down soon!" comforted Mr. Guru.

Truly enough, the strands of flames arched downward and plunged back into the sun's surface and the animals' spaceship came down with it. The three animals looked up and were astounded by the sight of this unearthly explosion.

"Mr. Guru, we're witnessing the most awesome sight we've ever seen in our lives!" started Happa. "A gigantic gas flame shot up like a forceful geyser. Then it bent and formed an arch and came down to the sun's surface! Our spaceship also came down with it. That arch is still floating high above the sun's surface! It looks like a magnificent flaming arch! Isn't that amazing?"

"We did flame-surfing, Mr. Guru! It was just like riding on the waves of the ocean with a surf board! It was scary, but exciting!" said Finny excitedly.

"You're seeing one of the sun's most spectacular fireworks! It's called the **prominence** eruption. These explosions start in the chromosphere and shoot out through the corona, throwing large blobs of gas into space. The loops of fiery gas hang high above the sun for days, weeks, or sometimes months, supported by the sun's magnetic field. Some of the prominences are over 100,000 miles in height and about 3,000 miles in width," explained Mr. Guru.

"Now, you are entering the third layer of the sun called the photosphere or the light sphere (photo means "light"). This is the region which we see from Earth every day."

The animals' spaceship slowly entered the third layer of the sun. The three animals were excited to get such a close-up view of the surface of the sun, but they were glad to be in their spaceship when they looked at the thermometer— the temperature in the photosphere was about $11,000^0$ Fahrenheit. The animals could see black patches on the surface of the sun. They kept gazing at the sun's bright surface with undivided attention.

"Hey, look! The surface of the sun looks smooth from Earth, but it isn't smooth at all! In fact, it looks like the photosphere is made out of bits and pieces of rice!" Finny cried out in surprise.

"How neat! It looks like a mosaic," said Happa.

"You are both right; it sure does look that way," said Chalu, "but with one difference— that mosaic or those pieces of rice look like they're rising and falling! The whole area seems to be bubbling! The entire photosphere is one big bubbling pot of hot porridge! Mr. Guru, why does the sun look so different from Earth?"

"First of all, Chalu, you shouldn't look for these features of the sun from Earth without a special telescope. If you stare at the sun directly with the naked eye, it can blind you. In any case, those bits and pieces of rice of the photosphere are actually hot gas cells called **granules**. They're only visible through powerful telescopes," Mr. Guru explained.

The granules and the dark patches on the granules began to look enormous as the spaceship got closer.

"Wow! Look at those granules now!" shouted Chalu. "It's unbelievable!" These granules look so huge now!"

"Yes, those granules are super huge!" Mr. Guru said. "Some of these granules are about 187 to 625 miles in diameter."

"And...and, look at those dark patches on those granules! Those look huge too! They look like ink blotches and they're all different sizes and shapes. Boy, some of them are gigantic! It's funny that all those dark patches are in pairs or in groups!"

"Those black patches are craters, you dummy," said Finny confidently, "just like the craters on the moon. Isn't that right, Mr. Guru?"

"Those dark patches you are seeing are called the **sunspots**," Mr. Guru replied, "The magnetic storm inside the sun's interior gives rise to the sunspots on the solar disk. Sunspots always appear in pairs or in groups. The smallest sunspot you see is as big as the Earth. These are cooler regions on the surface of the sun and so they look darker."

"Cooler regions!" Finny spluttered. "Mr. Guru, right now, we're next to a sunspot and our spaceship's thermometer reads 7,000° Fahrenheit! That's what you call cool?"

"Oh, no! Don't misunderstand me. I meant cooler compared to the other areas of the photosphere," explained Mr. Guru.

"Sunspots were first noticed by a Chinese astronomer, and later observed by an Italian scientist named **Galileo** in the year 1610, with the help of his newly-invented telescope. Sometimes, a large number of sunspots pop up on the disk of the sun, and at other times only a few. This sunspot activity follows a cycle of 11 years; this is called the **sunspot cycle**. During the period of increased sunspot activity, flare outbursts become more common." Mr. Guru finished explaining.

"It's funny to think," said Chalu in a humorous voice, "that the sun gets blemishes or pimples just like people!"

"Yes, even the glorious sun gets zits," chuckled Mr. Guru.

All of a sudden there was a tremendous outburst near a large sunspot. Huge flames of raging gas exploded out, spreading up high like an inferno, sending intense light and heat millions of miles into space. The three animals' hearts skipped a few beats and the light and thunderous noise made them temporarily blind and deaf. They stood inside the spaceship, watching the explosion with their eyes popping out of their heads. This violent explosion lasted for only a few minutes. The three animals finally came back to their senses and then, Finny started with a stutter,

"Mr. G-g-g-g-g-uru, tha...tha...that explosion we just saw was a thousand times scarier than the previous one. Is this one of the sun's most powerful firework displays, or is there something bigger yet to come?" asked Chalu.

"You just saw the **flare** explosion, one of the largest explosions in the solar system! This violent explosion is the equivalent of detonating ten million hydrogen bombs! It sends intense radiation and atomic particles into space, which travel as far as the Earth and beyond," explained Mr. Guru.

"Good lord! This is too much! Let's get out of here fast!" cried the three animals in unison.

"You can't leave now! Your voyage through the sun is not yet complete, until you visit the interior of the sun," said Mr. Guru. "Just like the outer layers, the sun's interior is divided into three main parts. They are: the **Convective Zone**, the **Radiative Zone**, and the **Core**, or the center. From the photosphere, you'll be traveling into the convective zone first, to see how energy of the sun is transferred from the underlying layer to its surface," Mr. Guru explained.

The animals' spaceship slowly glided into the convective zone. It was an extremely turbulent area. Hot cells of gas were rising upward and the cold cells of gas were coming down, getting reheated and traveling upward again in an endless cycle. It was similar to the bubbling process inside a pot of hot water.

"Wow, this is exciting!" shouted the three animals. "We didn't know that heat was transported like this!"

"You saw convection, a process of energy transport. Convection takes place inside hot liquids and gases. The energy is transported from the hotter to the colder regions by this process. The sun's energy is transferred from the underlying layer to its surface in a vertical movement by circulating currents." explained Mr. Guru.

The Interior Layers of the Sun

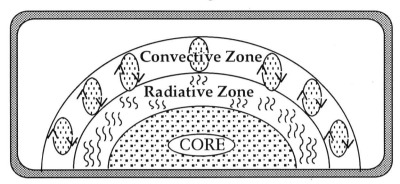

"Energy can travel by **convection**, **radiation** and **conduction**," continued Mr. Guru. "Convection is the transfer of energy by currents of gas or liquid. Radiation is energy transfer as waves or particles, like the sunlight which travels in the vacuum of space; and conduction is energy transfer by contact, such as when you sit in a hot bath tub and your body gets heated up by contact with the hot water."

3 ways of heat transfer

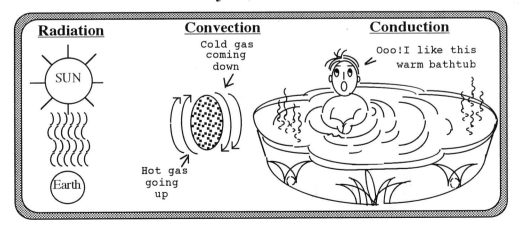

The spaceship slowly moved toward the radiative zone, where there was a high degree of radiation. The temperature and pressure inside the radiative zone was tremendously high.

"Mr. Guru," said Finny, "We don't see any convection or 'bubbling' happening in this region. How does the sun's energy move out from here?"

"First of all, there's a high density of energy concentrated in the radiative zone and the temperature level stays somewhat constant. The best way for the energy to travel upward from here is in the form of radiation, that is— as waves," explained Mr. Guru.

The animals' spaceship entered the core of the sun: the last and the final stop on their solar voyage. The core was huge! It was so dense, so hot, and so bright that the three animals couldn't find any words to describe it. The temperature was almost 29 million degrees Fahrenheit! Teeny tiny point-like particles were densely packed inside the core. The animals' spaceship made its way in at a very, very slow speed. It was the most frightening experience the three animals ever had in their lifetime. The core was like a giant powerhouse, generating light and heat.

"Whoa...Look at that!" fumbled Happa. "Look at those tiny energetic light-flashes everywhere!"

"Man, this is absolutely an impossible place to be in! It is too stuffy in here and it's terribly suffocating! I don't like it in here," cried out Finny anxiously. "Mr. Guru, Please take us out of this place. I'm afraid that, in this tight squeeze, we might blend with these particles and turn into energy!"

"Don't you worry, Finny! You all will be out of that place pretty soon. But first, I would like to explain the activities inside the sun's core. The core of the sun is as big as the planet Jupiter. Most of the point-like particles you see inside the core are hydrogen atoms. An atom is the smallest particle of matter. These hydrogen atoms are so densely packed in the core that they smash into each other and blend or fuse, and change into helium. In the process, energy is released. It is the same process by which a hydrogen bomb explodes. The radiation from inside the sun's core takes millions of years to make its way out to its surface, even at the speed of light, whereas the light from the sun's surface only takes eight minutes to reach the Earth," Mr. Guru explained.

"Then hurry up and take us out of here," Finny said in a panicky voice. "Otherwise, even in the form of energy, it'll take us forever to get out of this place! We've had enough of this place! We want out of the sun altogether!"

"Yes! Get us out of here!" the animals cried out in unison.

The next thing they knew, their spaceship was out of the sun's core and zooming through the radiative zone, convective zone, photosphere, chromosphere and finally, the coronal hole out into space. The animals found their spaceship racing forward with the solar wind, along with millions of glittering particles.

"Wheeee...Wheeee..." shouted the animals inside the spaceship. "We're being blown out with the solar wind of energetic particles!"

"Man, those particles are so tiny!" said Finny.

"They sure are!" cried out Happa and Chalu together.

"Hey, look!" said Happa. "We're heading for the Earth!"

"That's great!" shouted Finny and Chalu. "We're homeward bound at last!"

As their spaceship approached the Earth, they found lots of those energetic particles were deflected and trapped inside a donut-shaped ring.

"Hey, look! There is a huge donut-shaped jail around the Earth! It's holding the charged particles prisoner!" Finny said in a panic. "Oh no! We're also heading towards that jail! What should we do? Help, Mr. Guru!"

"Help! Help! Mr. Guru!" the animals shouted in a panic.

"You're not going to be trapped in there," said Mr. Guru. "You are not particles! That donut-shaped ring is Earth's **magnetosphere**. The magnetosphere is the area around a star or a planet which holds its magnetic field. The atomic particles are trapped by the magnetism of this region. The moon does not have a magnetic field like the Earth. Scientists believe that it could be due to the moon having a very small or no liquid iron core.

Van Allen Radiation Belts

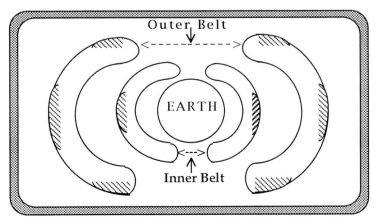

"There are two such donut-shaped areas, which are like protective shields around our planet. The harmful atomic particles coming from the sun or from outer space get trapped inside these two belts. These two belts are known as the **Van Allen radiation belts** because they were named after their discoverer, an astrophysicist named James Van Allen.

"The one you see now is the outer belt, which is located at about 13,700 miles above the Earth. The other one is the inner belt which is about 190 miles, just above the Earth's surface. These belts are Earth's high-radiation zones. Precautionary measures are taken by astronauts when traveling through these radiation zones." Mr. Guru finished explaining.

As the animals' spaceship continued its progress, the three animal astronauts saw that the energetic particles that had escaped the first belt were captured by the inner belt. There were still some particles which escaped both belts; as these particles descended down through the polar region, the sky lit up with shimmering red and green colors.

"Wow, look!" said Finny. "The sky is glowing with brilliant colors!" The three animals were spellbound. As they watched, the entire sky filled with swaying curtains of colorful lights.

"Mr. Guru, what's happening to the polar sky? Why is it so colorful?" asked Finny, but there was no answer.

"Mr. Guru, can you hear us?" asked Happa. Still there was no answer. "Oh no! Our communication system is messed up! Our compass is messed up, too— the needle is spinning wildly! What do we do now?" continued Happa, in a frightened voice. "Mr. Guru, please speak to us! Without your advice, we are lost! Please help us! We don't know what's happening!"

"Help! Help! Help!" the three animals cried.

"When I snap my fingers you will wake up," Mr. Guru's voice was heard. "Now you are back! You're back on the moon again."

Happa, Finny, and Chalu opened their eyes and found themselves sitting outside the lunar module with Mr. Guru in front of them.

"What an adventure we had! We'll never forget that trip," said the animals. "But what happened towards the end of our voyage? Why couldn't we talk to you at the end of our solar voyage?" asked Finny.

"Well, let me explain it to you," Mr. Guru started. "The colorful light display you saw in the polar sky is called **Aurora**— named after the Roman goddess of dawn. It happens when the electrically charged particles from outer space or the sun enter the polar regions and come in contact with the upper atmosphere of the Earth. The molecules in the atmosphere get excited with the touch of these charged particles and glow with multi-colored lights— mainly, red and green— in the polar sky. This light display has many captivating sequences, like curtains of colored lights as you saw, or like a half-circular fan, and so on. These displays can last for minutes or hours. Around the northern polar regions, the aurora is called the **Aurora Borealis** or 'northern dawn,' and around the southern polar regions, it's called **Aurora Australis** or 'southern dawn.'

"Besides creating the colorful display, these charged particles create disturbances in radio, TV, and telephone transmissions on Earth. I wanted you to experience some of the disturbance caused by these charged particles, so that you will remember it," explained Mr. Guru. "You can see that traveling to the sun would be a suicide mission. Even trying to approach the sun at a distance of several thousand miles would mean a fiery death to us all," concluded Mr. Guru.

"Thank you Mr. Guru for teaching us a lesson about the sun," said the animal astronauts. "We really enjoyed the hypnotic trip, even though it was kind of scary for us."

"Now come inside the module. It is time to eat dinner and take a rest," Mr. Guru said.

"But Mr. Guru," Finny complained, "the sun is still shining. There's still plenty of daylight! We'd all like to wait until the sun goes down before we go to bed."

"Well, for your information, the sun does not set here on the moon for fourteen days! It is unlike the Earth, where the day and night cycle is 24 hours. On the moon, the day and night cycle is 28 Earth days— fourteen days of daylight and fourteen days of night. So, you fellows have to wait a long time for that nap. Suit yourselves, but I am turning in right now." With these words, Mr. Guru disappeared into the module.

The animals were shocked by Mr. Guru's account of the day and night cycle on the moon.

"Fourteen days of light and fourteen days of darkness--- that is unbelievable!" said Finny.

"Unbelievable, but true," said Chalu. "I can't keep awake for that long! I'm turning in. See you later!" Chalu went inside the module.

Happa and Finny quickly followed Mr. Guru and the three animal astronauts finished their meals and curled up inside the module to get some sleep.

Chapter 9

The Mystery of the Missing Rabbit

After a while, Chalu woke up and found everybody sleeping peacefully, except, that is, for Happa, who was missing from her sleeping place.

"Where is Happa?" Chalu asked, as he stood up with a bounce. He looked all over for the rabbit, but couldn't find hide nor hair of her. Chalu panicked and woke Mr. Guru and Finny. All of them searched every corner of the module, then peeked outside. There wasn't a trace of Happa. Finny was very frightened by Happa's disappearance and whispered to Chalu,

"I don't know about you, but I was pretty suspicious of this place from the moment we set foot on it! I was sure that there were some creepy creatures hiding around inside the craters or behind the mountains. Those creatures are everywhere, just waiting to eat us for dinner. Can you imagine a place this size having nothing other than rocks and sand? No, Sir! I bet a long time ago, the moon was hustling and bustling with people, animals, and plants. There were meadows and green valleys, waterfalls, and huge rivers all over the moon. These craters were once reservoirs or lakes filled with crystal-clear sparkling water! I bet one can still find water inside some of these deep craters. In any case, there were jungles on the moon with lush green trees loaded with plump fruits and fragrant flowers.

"Then the whole scene changed drastically when these unknown creatures showed up, God only knows from where! They devoured and destroyed everything on the moon's surface, turning this place into a desert full of rubble. Then, when they'd eaten everything they could find, they made these craters and rayed craters by scratching with their sharp claws to dig for food and water! You know what? When I was trying to sleep, I could hear spooky hissing sounds, cracking and gurgling noises coming from outside. I bet those sounds were made by those moon-creatures! Undoubtedly, they are the prime suspect in Happa's disappearance!" Finny paused for a moment and started again.

"Poor Happa! No one knows what kind of torture and pain she might be going through as a prisoner of those hideous creatures! She might be crying out for help, calling us by our names! 'Finneeee! Chaloooo! My friends! Please help me!' Oh, dear! Happa might be lying on one of the creature's dinner tables as we speak! How horrible! I can't talk about it anymore!" Finny couldn't help sobbing aloud and Chalu joined him.

"Stop this nonsense this instant," Mr. Guru snapped. "It is silly for grownups like yourselves to cry like kids over imaginary problems! All we know is that Happa is missing. It doesn't mean that she's dead or even in trouble! I must say, Finny has a very vivid imagination! How could there be any life form here on the moon without air and water? Suppose we assume that some such hungry creatures live on the moon and they took Happa for their meal. Why didn't they bag us as well? Why would they pass up fried fish, baked crow, and barbecued owl?" Mr. Guru asked.

"Because the creatures didn't want to mix up the tastes or finish the food supply at one go! They're saving us for their next meal," Finny said promptly. "Our turn will come soon!"

"Finny, I must admit you not only have a vivid imagination, you also have pretty good explanations," Mr. Guru said, smiling. "I assure you that no such creatures exist up here on the moon."

"How could you say so, Mr. Guru?!" snapped Finny. "I heard them clearly, outside, making noises! They were hissing, gurgling and trying to crack open our spacecraft!"

"Oh, no," Mr. Guru laughed. "Those noises were coming out of our spacecraft due to extreme heat. Our spacecraft is made out of metals and when the metals are heated, they expand and produce such noises. As far as Happa is concerned, my guess is that she must have stepped out for a moment to enjoy the moonscape or to jog and exercise in the open. You two, put on your space suits and go look for Happa."

Chalu and Finny stopped crying, got dressed, and headed out to look for Happa with Mr. Guru. All three searched everywhere, even behind rocks and inside craters. Then they looked as far as they could see through their binoculars. They called for Happa through their helmet's radios but without success. There was no sign of Happa anywhere. Time passed, and Mr. Guru got together with Finny and Chalu to make a decision and devise a different search plan. Suddenly they spotted a figure from a distance, and it slowly advanced toward them.

"Let's hurry and get inside the module!" said the frightened Finny. "Here comes one of the moon creatures. I bet he's coming to get his next meal!" Before he got too far, though, the figure came closer and everyone could see him clearly.

"Look who's coming! It's our friend, Happa!" Chalu shouted excitedly. "Thank God for bring Happa back in one piece!"

Chalu and Finny cheered Happa as she neared, but Mr. Guru was silent and seemed a bit upset.

"It's totally irresponsible of you to take off in that sneaky way without informing us," said Mr. Guru. "You have no idea what you've put us through! We were worried sick and searched for you for hours!"

"I'm really sorry for putting you through all that trouble," said Happa. "I had no intention of doing that! I was sure that I'd be back before you all awoke, but I misjudged the time. In any case, my mission was a failure." Happa seemed depressed.

"What mission?" asked Mr. Guru. "Or would you rather not talk about it?"

"Oh, I don't mind telling you about it," Happa said. "The purpose of my mission was to find the 'moon god' and his 'pet rabbit' who live here on the moon. I walked a long way looking for them, but there was no trace of them. I guess they might be farther away than I thought, or maybe they're invisible."

Mr. Guru couldn't hold back his laughter. "I can't believe my ears! You really went out to look for these storybook characters the 'moon god' and his 'pet rabbit?' I'm surprised at you, Happa! You have come to the moon as an astronaut and still believe in those stories? They have no scientific basis! There are many such stories in other parts of the world about a girl on the moon and a man on the moon. These stories are created by people's imaginations. Just as you see the imprint of a rabbit on the moon, those people see the imprints of a girl wearing a necklace or the big face of a man! These stories are fun to read but the truth is, you're all seeing craters, maria, and the mountains on the moon. With a bit of imagination, these start to resemble a rabbit, a girl or a man's face from Earth.

"Likewise, earlier in history, people thought that the phases of the moon were caused by hungry space creatures, because they believed that the moon was made out of white cheese! You've all seen that the moon is not made out of cheese; it's basically made out of the same ingredients as the Earth, such as rocks and sand."

"Mr. Guru," interrupted Chalu. "The story you just told about the moon being eaten up by space creatures reminded me of a Hindu myth I once heard. In the story, there are two demons named Rahu and Ketu. The demon Rahu is only a head without a body and the demon Ketu is only a body without a head. These two demons swallow the sun or the moon, causing darkness on Earth for a while. Then the sun and the moon slip out through the demons' throat or body within minutes.

Rahu swallowing the Sun

"I have also witnessed such events a couple of times from Earth! I will tell you my own experience of one such event when the sun was swallowed by one of these two demons, causing temporary darkness on Earth," Chalu continued. Once, under a midday sun, I was lunching on a delicious ripe papaya when I sensed something strange, something evil in the air! The sunlight was slowly diminishing. I looked up. There was not a cloud in the sky, but to my surprise, I found the sun was slowly disappearing into

The animals' lunar module is taking off from the moon. (see page 85)

Our Solar System

something dark and mysterious! Daylight faded away and a sudden chill swept across the woods replacing the heat of the midday sun.

"The flowers closed their petals. The birds and the animals stopped chitter-chattering. A sudden silence descended upon the woods. It made my feathers stand on end all over my body. In a few minutes, the sun was completely gone from the sky. All the animals and birds, including me, cuddled inside our homes to settle down, thinking that night had approached. The night animals crawled out of their hiding places and started to hunt for food. I even noticed a few stars twinkling in the sky! Then, to my surprise and everyone else's, daylight suddenly started to return! Within a few minutes, the sun was back in the sky and shining with full glory! I realized then that it was one of the demons Rahu or Ketu who was responsible for the sun's disappearance. I also saw a similar thing happened on a moonlit night, when the moon disappeared and reappeared minutes later."

"Hey Chalu! Please tell us the story about those demons. We'd like to hear it!" Finny said excitedly.

"Yes, I'd love to hear the demon story, too. It sounds interesting!" added Happa.

"Go ahead! Tell the story! We'd all like to hear it," Mr. Guru said.

"All right," said Chalu. "I'll tell the story. This story is from the mythology of India."

"Lord Brahma created the universe and many worlds inside it, including our Earth. He also created all the living things on Earth, like people, animals, birds, and insects. Brahma also created many mini gods called Devas. They were the sun god, the moon god, the rain god, the wind god, and many more to assist him. The rain god was chosen to be the king of the mini gods. In the course of time, many demons were also born. These demons were very strong and evil by nature. They terrorized the heaven and the Earth. They were never on good terms with the mini gods. Most of the time, the demons picked fights with the mini gods, for power and dominance. It was like a battle between good and evil.

Once, the demons attacked and occupied the heaven. They drove all the mini gods away, along with their king. The mini gods approached Lord Vishnu, the supreme power in the universe, for help. Lord Vishnu wanted the mini gods to be stronger than the demons and become immortal! So he asked them to drink 'Amrit,' a divine nectar which was kept hidden inside an ocean named 'Milk Ocean.'

The 'Milk Ocean' was vast and deep. The mini gods decided to churn the 'Milk Ocean' using an ancient method that was used to make butter in olden days. The method was as follows: First, a wooden rod with fan-like blades on one end was placed inside the milk. Then a piece of string was wrapped tightly around the middle of the rod with two loose ends hanging out. The milk was churned by pulling alternately on the two loose ends with both hands."

"Why did the mini gods try such a primitive method of taking the nectar of immortality out of the Milk Ocean?" Happa interrupted.

"I think in those days, they didn't have scuba gear, otherwise they'd have dove to the bottom of the ocean in their wet suits," Chalu said sarcastically.

"But the gods should've been able to do anything they wanted! They're supposed to have magical powers! Besides, Lord Vishnu could have found the Amrit easily. He was the supreme power," Happa insisted.

"I guess these gods had limited magical powers, since they were only mini gods. Lord Vishnu didn't get the Amrit because he wanted the mini gods to work hard so they'd really appreciate it when they did find it," Chalu explained.

"That was a pretty good explanation, Chalu," praised Mr. Guru.

"Anyway, back to the story," Chalu continued.

"To churn a vast and deep ocean, the mini gods needed a super tall churner and a super long rope. They decided to use the tallest mountain as their churning rod and the longest snake as the churning rope. The mini gods found it difficult to churn such a huge ocean all by themselves. They needed help, but the only other beings strong enough to do the job were the demons. The mini gods decided they'd have to ask the demons for help, but the only way they could convince the evil devils to help was by promising to share the salvaged treasures including Amrit with them.

The mini gods and the demons placed the mountain inside the Milk Ocean, with the snake wrapped around it like a rope. The mini gods held the snake's tail and the demons held its head. Lord Vishnu transformed himself into a giant turtle and helped carry the mountain on his back to keep it floating. Then the churning of the Milk Ocean began. Many treasures were salvaged out of the Milk Ocean, including a super fast divine horse, a divine elephant with six trunks, a divine flower with everlasting freshness and fragrance, and a group of most beautiful divine dancers. Most of all, 'Laxmi,' the goddess of wealth and prosperity, appeared from inside the Milk Ocean. The mini gods were so excited that they claimed all these treasures and took them away. This made the demons very, very angry.

'Hey! What's going on here? We've been ripped off! It's not fair!' growled one demon. 'We should do something about it!'

'Yes! We must take action!' thundered another.

'Patience, my friends! Let's hang on a bit longer till Amrit, the nectar of immortality, comes out. Then we will take action,' the leader of the demons said.

The ocean continued to churn. Finally, the divine medicine man appeared from inside the Milk Ocean with a jug of Amrit in his hand. A loud cheer arose from the demons. They quickly abandoned their churning, dashed towards the medicine man, and snatched the jug of Amrit from his hand. All the demons climbed up the mountain and prepared to drink the Amrit, all by themselves. The mini gods were helpless and frustrated. In desperation, they prayed to Lord Vishnu for help. In answer to the mini gods' prayers, Vishnu transformed himself into the most beautiful maiden in the universe and appeared at the churning site with a jug of wine in her hand.

All the demons came crashing down the mountain towards the maiden and surrounded her like swarms of bees around a flower. The maiden's extraordinary beauty and heart-winning smile captivated the mini gods and the demons alike, but the mini gods knew the maiden's true identity, whereas the demons didn't. The demons began to swarm her with questions.

'Where are you from, pretty maiden?' asked one demon

'What's your name, doll?' asked another.

'How about a little kiss, honey bun?' asked the next one.

'How about you and I getting married, sugar plum?' said the fourth.

Mohini and the demons

The maiden smiled and spoke softly, 'I am Mohini. My name means 'enchantress.' I have come from far away and I happened to pass by this way, when I noticed you boys having some kind of party! I love parties! Moreover, you all looked so handsome and strong that I had to come over. I simply adore macho guys like you! I would love to serve you all. Let me have that jug and you boys just sit down and enjoy yourselves while I pour.'

With these words, Mohini took the jug of Amrit from one of the demons. The demons were so enchanted by the beauty of this maiden that they couldn't take their eyes off her. They couldn't refuse her request and did exactly as she told them, which was to sit down with their enemies, the mini gods. The demons and the mini gods formed two separate groups and sat down. Now, Mohini started serving the mini gods first, pouring Amrit into their cups and wine into the demons. The demons were too busy watching Mohini to pay any attention to their drinks.

In the meantime, a demon named Rahu disguised himself as a mini god and switched places. No one had noticed him do this, except the sun and the moon gods. They quickly pointed out the demon to Lord Vishnu who was disguised as Mohini. Lord Vishnu instantly deployed his weapon called Sudarshan, a disk-shaped blade, and cut off the demon Rahu's head. But Rahu didn't die, because he had already sipped in the immortal nectar. Instead, Rahu's head and his body became two separate live demons. The head was called Rahu as before, and the body was called Ketu.

These two demons, Rahu and Ketu, were outraged by the action of the sun and the moon gods. They tried to chase and catch the sun and the moon gods from that time onward. Sometimes these two demons, Rahu and Ketu, catch up with the sun or the moon god and swallow them in revenge, but the sun and the moon slip out through the openings of these two demons' cut head and body. That is the reason why the eclipse of the sun or the moon takes place." Chalu finished his story.

"I don't deny these events of the solar or the lunar eclipses, Chalu," said Mr. Guru. "It is true that sometimes the sun and the moon pass through these phases, but it's not because demons like Rahu or Ketu are swallowing them. People in China and several tribes in some of the Islands have stories similar to this one. They believe that a ferocious dragon swallows the sun and the moon, causing darkness on Earth. During that period, these people try to scare off the dragon by producing loud sounds with different musical instruments, such as drums and cymbals.

"The scientific truth behind these events is totally different. The disappearance of the sun or the moon is caused by an eclipse— the blocking of light by one body or the other. It's like the head of a tall person blocking your view in a movie theater. Let me explain it to you. The moon is moving around the Earth and the Earth around the sun. Occasionally these three bodies line up, causing eclipses on the Earth.

"Sometimes the moon lies between the sun and the Earth, blocking our view of the sun from Earth. This is called an eclipse of the sun (partial or total) or a **solar eclipse**. A solar eclipse lasts for a very short period, less than eight minutes, because of the continuing motion and the small size of the moon.

Solar Eclipse

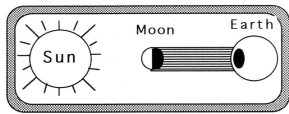

"At other times, when the moon passes into the Earth's shadow an eclipse of the moon (partial or total) or a **lunar eclipse** (luna means "moon" in Latin) takes place. A lunar eclipse lasts longer, for about forty minutes or so, because the Earth is larger in size and casts a larger shadow on the moon. During a lunar eclipse, the moon looks reddish in color, instead of disappearing completely from view.

Lunar Eclipse

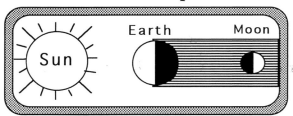

"The moon doesn't get smaller from some space creature's hungry bites. The varying shapes of the moon happen due to the moon's orbit around the Earth and the relative reflection of the sunlight from its surface. The moon does not have its own light like the Earth. It reflects light from the sun. The varying shapes of the moon is called the 'phases of the moon.'

"The moon moves round the Earth in 28 days, but from Earth, we see the phases of the moon repeating over a period of 30 days. So the phases of the moon follow a cycles of 29 and half or 30 days. The first-half of this cycle is known as the **waxing stage** and the second-half is known as the **waning stage** of the moon.

"During the waxing phase, the moon progresses from *new moon* (no moon) to a *crescent moon* to a *quarter moon, half moon* then to a *gibbous moon* (humpback) and finally it becomes a *full moon*. During the waning phase, the lighted portions of the moon decrease gradually starting from full moon size, back to a gibbous, half, then to a quarter and to a crescent, ending in no moon.

Phases of the Moon

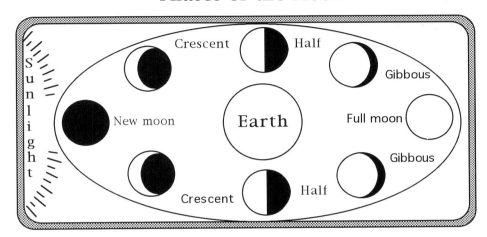

"The moon takes the same time to travel around the Earth as it takes to go around its own axis, that is— 28 days. That's why we see the same lighted side of the moon from the Earth all the time."

"Mr. Guru," interrupted Finny. "If we lived on the far-side of the moon, we would never be able to see the Earth, ever! Isn't that right?"

"You are right Finny," said Mr. Guru. "The Earth is not visible from the far-side of the moon. Anyway, people had no idea about the opposite side of the moon that we couldn't see— the far-side of the moon— until NASA deployed several moon probes with cameras and other devices and collected a lot of data about the opposite side of the moon. From the photographs, it was confirmed that the far-side of the moon is heavily cratered but has no really big craters like those on the visible side. Also, the far side has no maria. Scientists still puzzle over the dissimilarity between the two sides of the moon," Mr. Guru explained.

"Mr. Guru," Happa started enthusiastically. "I was wondering; where did the moon come from and how did it become our Earth's satellite?"

"Yes, we were wondering about it too!" cried out Chalu and Finny together.

"That's a good question," said Mr. Guru. "There are a number of theories about the origin of the moon. Among them, scientists favor one theory which states that when the Earth was very young, it was hot and molten. A huge celestial body— one third of the size of our Earth (about the size of Mars), collided with the young Earth. As a result, debris or chunks from the Earth were thrown out into its orbit. This debris combined together and formed the Earth's moon. Now, astronauts! We have finished the rest of our assignments and get ready to leave!" Mr. Guru concluded and went inside the module.

Chapter 10

A Farewell to the Moon

"**Fellows**! I just talked to the human astronauts of Apollo 11 on the moon through my two-way radio," said Mr. Guru cheerfully, as he came down the ladder of the lunar module. "But I didn't mention to them anything about our problem of abandoning our command module at a lunar orbit, because I thought we should try to handle it by ourselves. If we don't succeed, I will request NASA's help!"

"You did the right thing, Mr. Guru!" said the animal astronauts. "One must try to solve one's own problems, as far as possible!"

"Anyway, I would like to brief you on the activities of the human astronauts on the moon. First, they planted a three-by-five-foot nylon flag of the United States on the lunar soil. It's not easy to fly a flag in the absence of the air! The flag will just droop down instead of flying. So the flag taken by the astronauts to the moon had a wire attached on the top edge to keep it extended on the airless moon.

"They had also begin to run a series of lunar experiments on the moon's surface, which were sent up with the astronauts by scientists on Earth. One of these experiments was a **laser reflector experiment**, which would measure the exact distance of the moon from the Earth. The second one was a **solar experiment** to catch or collect cosmic and gamma rays coming out of the sun by exposing a piece of aluminum foil to the lunar sun. The third and the last of the experiments was an instrument called a **seismometer**, to study the activities of the moon's interior such as: moonquakes, volcanic eruption, or meteorite impact. The astronauts also have collected a sample of moon rocks— about 50 pounds worth— and have scooped a fair amount of moon soil in a collection bag to carry back to Earth for scientific studies."

"Mr. Guru," interrupted Happa, "could we take a few samples of moon rocks and a bit of moon dust back as souvenirs?"

"Of course you may! Those would be the most valuable souvenirs anybody could ever have!" the wise owl said. He brought a collecting bag and a scooper and handed them to the animals. "Get busy and collect your souvenirs. There isn't much time."

The three animal astronauts started running around grabbing moon rocks of different sizes and textures and also scooped up some moon soil. In the meantime, Mr. Guru went inside the module and brought out a rectangular **plaque** made of stainless steel. It had some writing on it and Mr. Guru asked the animals to read it. The animals read out loud,

'Here, animals from the planet Earth first set foot upon the moon in July, 1969 AD. We came in peace for all the animal species.' Signed...

Astronaut Happa Hooper (Rabbit)— Representative of land animals.

Astronaut Finny Flapper (Fish)— Representative of water animals.

Astronaut Chalu Chacha (Crow)— Representative of airborne animals.

Mr. Guru Maharaj (Owl)— The counselor to the animal astronauts.

All three animal astronauts applauded and cheered loudly while Mr. Guru attached the plaque to the legs of the descent stage.

"The human astronauts of Apollo 11 have unveiled a plaque similar to ours with a little variation in size and inscription," announced Mr. Guru. "Their plaque says,

'Here, men from planet Earth first set foot on the moon. July, 1969 AD. We came in peace for all mankind.'

"The signatures of Apollo 11 astronauts— Neil Armstrong, Michael Collins and Edwin Aldrin are engraved on that plaque. Also, the signature of the president of the United States, Richard Nixon, is there on that plaque.

"Now, we have ended our moon expedition," said Mr. Guru. "We should make arrangements to get back home to Earth. Follow me!"

Mr. Guru went back inside the lunar module with the three animals following behind him. All of them settled down inside the cabin. The wise owl started throwing some items out of the module. He got rid of all the pairs of lunar boots, a couple of backpacks, a couple of space suits, and a camera.

"Mr. Guru! What are you doing?" Happa cried. "Why are you throwing away those expensive and necessary items?"

"Normally, I wouldn't throw them away, but I have to make sure that our lunar module is light enough for lift-off. Besides, we have no need for those things anymore," explained Mr. Guru. "Apollo 11 astronauts did the same thing as I did".

All three animal astronauts settled down in their seats and buckled their seat belts. The wise owl lifted up the ladder and closed the hatch of the lunar module. He tightly sealed and pressurized the cabin. Then he checked out the operational switches to make sure that they were in working order. Then he ignited the booster engine to lift the lunar module from the moon's surface. The spacecraft slowly rose, climbing higher and higher into space, leaving behind its **descent stage** (base of the lunar module). The three animals glanced down at the moon for the last time and said good-bye.

"I feel sad to leave the moon even though I am more excited to go back home to Earth," Chalu said. "We have left behind all those stuff! Maybe some visitors from another planet will find them some day and wonder about the owners."

"We not only left those articles behind, but we also left our footprints on the lunar soil. Those will last for hundreds and thousands of years because, on the moon, there is no rain to wash them away and no wind to blow them away," Mr. Guru explained.

"I think we should have left a couple of pictures of ourselves along with the other stuff. Then visitors from other planets would know that we were not only intelligent creatures, but that we were pretty good-looking too," said Finny jokingly.

"Mr. Guru!" started Happa. "We thank you from the bottom of our hearts for being an excellent teacher and counselor on this moon mission. We enjoyed this trip thoroughly and also learned a lot."

"Yes, we all think so," joined the other two animals. "You were a terrific teacher!"

"I thank you all! I was just doing my duty!" said Mr. Guru, smiling.

The lunar module continued its climb, getting further and further away from the moon. The animals were overwhelmed with joy and excitement to see the big blue Earth hanging in space. It looked like a big blue and white marble. They wanted to go home fast. They had forgotten that they couldn't return to Earth without the command module, which was floating aimlessly around the moon without a pilot. Soon, the lunar module started orbiting around the moon. Mr. Guru spoke up.

"Now, we shall stay in this orbit for a while and try to catch hold of the command module. If we do catch it, we'll quickly get back in and return to the Earth. As you all know, we anticipated this situation. We didn't have any other alternative if we were to be the contemporary pioneers of men in this moon expedition. Let's give it a try!"

Mr. Guru tried his best to catch up with the command module and dock it with their lunar module. All his attempts failed. Time passed and the lunar module's booster rocket began to burn out. The red light indicating exhausted fuel supply started flashing. Chalu, Happa and Finny stared at the light with anxious pounding hearts.

"Well, well, so much for the lunar module. You all shouldn't look so worried," consoled Mr. Guru. "We tried our best. We would have tried a little longer if we had more fuel. The first thing I'm going to do is switch on the outside stress light. After that, I will report to NASA ground-control and request their help. You three just sit and watch," concluded Mr. Guru.

Mr. Guru got busy right away and did exactly as he said. He turned on the stress light and established contact with NASA's mission control through the two-way radio. He consulted with them for several minutes, then finally announced with a smile,

"Help is on the way! You astronauts take it easy and relax now!"

The three animals were scared to death of being stranded in space.

"What will happen to us if help doesn't arrive soon? We'll probably drift around here until we die without food, water, or oxygen! Or our spaceship might crash by the pull of moon's gravity!" said Finny anxiously.

"Darn! I should have settled down with a wife and a couple of kids." started Chalu. "I was a stubborn fool not to do so," Chalu sighed. "I miss Nishy so much! She was so sweet and so.o.o...beautiful! And...and..."

"Who is Nishy?" Finny interrupted.

"She was my girlfriend," said Chalu. "I still remember those wonderful days when Nishy and I used to sit together on a leafy branch of a tree, next to a river— chatting, joking and laughing. It was Nishy who proposed to me one day, instead of I! But I refused her, because I loved the idea of being a swinging bachelor and a daredevil! I walked through fire, flew through storms, and glided from the highest peaks! Man, I was such a fool not to say yes to her marriage proposal! Finally, like a fool, I volunteered for this dangerous mission to die without anyone left behind to carry on my name!" Chalu sighed.

"I know what you mean, Chalu!" started Finny. "I was a brat all through my childhood. I never joined a school of fish because I used to think that schools were for nerds! So, I never learned the lessons of how to survive in the dangerous water of the ocean. I used to roam around freely and do as I pleased! I poked my nose into everything and everywhere, big or small. I chased the sharks and teased the dangerous creatures of the deep. I was once caught inside a fisherman's net but luckily I was set free. A shark bit off a portion of my tail for my stupidity too. It was a narrow escape but even that didn't teach me a lesson.

"My mother used to warn me, saying, 'Son, you'd better settle down, join the school and mind your own business, or else you won't live long enough to have fun!' She was so right, but I never paid any attention to her advice. I thought she was old-fashioned. Now I know that my mother was wise! I would kiss her a million times if she were here now!" Finny was depressed.

"You guys really tick me off!" yelled Happa. "You sit here lamenting over the past and it doesn't do a bit of good. You two started your lives as stubborn fools and you'll be fools till you die! You never listen to advice anyway! Look how much trouble you two caused on the moon when you ignored Mr. Guru's advice."

"Look who's talking— it is Miss Goody-goody, I guess," said Finny sarcastically. "You're no better than us, as far as listening to advice is concerned! You snuck out to look for the fictional characters like the 'moon god' and his 'pet rabbit' without Mr. Guru's permission. You just zip your mouth and sit down!" said Finny angrily.

"Now, now! Calm down! There's no need to quarrel like this. The help will be arriving soon and we all will be going back home! Right now, Let's think about something else. I know! This is the perfect time for you to learn **astronomy**, which means "*star arranging*" in Greek. A long time ago, the Greeks used to gaze at the stars and mentally arrange them in groups called **constellations**. Are you interested in learning about the stars and planets?" Mr. Guru asked.

"It's okay with us, Mr. Guru! We have no objections," the three animals said in unison.

"First, let's start with a *family* on Earth. A family consists of parents, children, grandparents, grandchildren, and so on. As we know, a family resides in a *village* or a *city*. A city is a part of a *state* and a state belongs to a *country*. Again, a country is a part of a *continent* which belongs to the *Earth*.

"For example, *X family* has a father, a mother and a child. This family lives in *Baltimore* (city) which is in *Maryland* (state). Maryland is a part of the *United States* (country). The United States is in *North America* (continent) which is a part of our *Earth*.

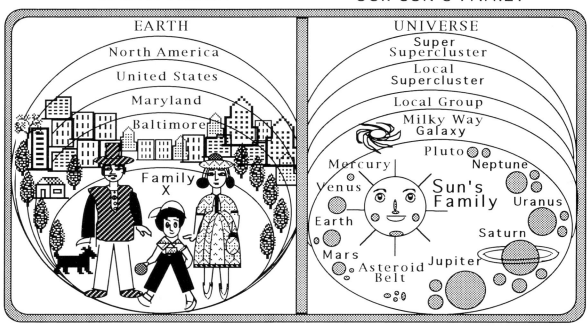

EARTH FAMILY   OUR SUN'S FAMILY

"Likewise, our sun has a family too! It's called the **Solar System**. The sun is the center of our solar system and nine known **planets** revolve around it. Planet means "wanderer" in Greek. These planets are like the sun's children. These nine planets have their own satellites or moons that go around them which are like the sun's grandchildren.

"Starting from the closest to the farthest, the names of the planets are as follows: **Mercury, Venus, Earth, Mars, Jupiter, Saturn, Uranus, Neptune,** and **Pluto**. Mercury and Venus have no moon. The Earth has one *moon*. Mars has 2 moons— *Deimos* and *Phobos*. Jupiter has 16 known moons. Some of the biggest moons of Jupiter are *Callisto, Io, Ganymede* and

Europa. Saturn has 24 known moons and some of their names are *Enceladus, Titan, Calypso, Mimas, Dione,* and *Rhea.* The planet Uranus has 15 known moons. Some among them are *Miranda, Ariel, Umbriel,* and *Oberon.* Neptune has 8 known moons, two of which are called *Triton* and *Nereid.* The ninth planet, Pluto, has one moon named *Sharon.*

"Besides these nine planets and their moons, thousands of **asteroids** orbit the sun in between the orbits of Mars and Jupiter. This is known as the **asteroid belt**. These asteroids are like minor or mini planets. They are mostly lumps of rock and metal, ranging from small pebbles to huge boulders. Also, there are countless numbers of meteoroids and comets that orbit the sun, which are also part of our solar system. All these celestial bodies are attracted by the gravitational force of the sun and stay in orbit around it. This is our sun's family. Our sun's family is only a tiny portion of the vast system called the **universe**. I would like to explain the position of our sun's family inside the vast framework of the universe." Mr. Guru explained.

"Mr. Guru, where is our sun's partner? To start with, a family has a father and a mother," Happa asked.

"Normally that is the case," said Mr. Guru. "Our sun's family is like a single-parent family. In any case, our sun with its 9 planets and 66 known moons resides in a huge *star city* known as a **galaxy**. A galaxy is a star system with millions of stars within it. Our sun's galaxy is called the **Milky Way**. The name Milky Way was given because only a small portion of this galaxy— a band of shinny white stars— is visible from the Earth and it looks like spilled milk.

"The Milky Way is shaped like a giant pinwheel. It's called a **spiral galaxy**. It has a luminous central hub and winding spiral arms made out of gas and dust. The size of the Milky Way is enormous! Even if we travel at the speed of light (18600 miles per second), which is the fastest speed known to us, it would take 100,000 years to go from one end of the galaxy to the other. Our sun family lives on one of the spiral arms of the Milky Way. Like our sun, there are about 200 billion stars in the Milky Way. Some may have families like our sun.

"The Milky Way is a part of a small group of galaxies called the **Local Group** (*star state*). This local group has about 30 galaxies. The largest one is **Andromeda** and our Milky Way is the second largest galaxy in that group.

"This local group is a part of a supercluster, called **Local Supercluster** (*star country*). Scientists believe this supercluster could be connected to a **Super-Supercluster** of galaxy which is like a *star continent*. This Super-supercluster is a part of the **universe**," Mr. Guru explained.

"Now, focusing on the universe, I will start with the creation of the universe. There are two main theories about the creation of the universe. The first theory is called the **Steady State** and the second theory is called the **Big Bang**. The Big Bang theory is the most widely accepted by astronomers and scientists all over the world. According to the Big Bang theory, some 10 to 20 billion years ago, the entire universe was stuffed inside a geometric point in the form of energy. This geometric point is called a **primordial atom** or a **primordial ball**. The extreme temperature and the pressure inside this primordial ball led to an explosion called the 'Big Bang.' With this explosion, the universe expanded and the foundation for the creation of matter was laid down," explained Mr. Guru.

It's a vast universe, a storehouse of many wonders and mysteries. Countless stars and galaxies extend up to billions of light years in space, and light up the face of the universe. The most distant objects like **quasars** shine with extraordinary luminosity. Lovely bright **nebulae**, the birthplaces of the stars, glow with brilliant colors. **Nova** outbursts resulting from the transfer of energy between two stars flare up, outshining even the brightest stars around. Spectacular **supernova** explosions end the lives of massive stars hurtling away the stars' contents into space in all directions. Pulsating **neutron stars** sweep across space with their light beams, like lighthouses on seashores. The bizarre **black holes** are like holes in space-time from which nothing can escape, not even the light! All these are parts of this amazing universe. I hope, after you get back to the Earth, you will try to learn more about these interesting celestial objects as well as the lives of the great scientists who have tried to reveal the beauty and truth about them."

"We will! We will!" shouted Happa, Chalu and Finny enthusiastically.

While listening to Mr. Guru, Finny the fish was sailing away on a voyage through the universe in a half-conscious sleep.